THE DRAMA WITH DOOMSDAYS

DON'T MISS THE START OF THE CELIA CLEARY SERIES:

The Problem with Prophecies

THE DRAMA WITH DOOMSDAYS

THE CELIA CLEARY SERIES

BOOK 2

SCOTT REINTGEN

ALADDIN
New York   London   Toronto   Sydney   New Delhi

ALADDIN

An imprint of Simon & Schuster Children's Publishing Division

1230 Avenue of the Americas, New York, New York 10020

First Aladdin hardcover edition May 2023

Text copyright © 2023 by Scott Reintgen

Jacket illustration copyright © 2023 by Julie McLaughlin

For information about special discounts for bulk purchases, please contact Simon & Schuster Special Sales at 1-866-506-1949 or business@simonandschuster.com. The Simon & Schuster Speakers Bureau can bring authors to your live event. For more information or to book an event, contact the Simon & Schuster Speakers Bureau at 1-866-248-3049 or visit our website at www.simonspeakers.com.

Designed by Laura Lyn DiSiena

The text of this book was set in Urge Text.

Manufactured in the United States of America 0423 FFG

2 4 6 8 10 9 7 5 3 1

Library of Congress Cataloging-in-Publication Data

Names: Reintgen, Scott, author.

Title: The drama with doomsdays / Scott Reintgen.

Description: First Aladdin hardcover edition. | New York, New York : Aladdin, 2023. | Series: The Celia Cleary series ; 2 | Audience: Ages 10 to 14. | Summary: "Eighth grader Celia has a strange vision that foretells a doomsday scenario for her school and suggests another seer is nearby"—Provided by publisher.

Identifiers: LCCN 2022053316 (print) | LCCN 2022053317 (ebook) | ISBN 9781665903608 (hardcover) | ISBN 9781665903622 (ebook)

Subjects: CYAC: Clairvoyance—Fiction. | Blessing and cursing—Fiction. | Charms—Fiction. | Magic—Fiction. | Schools—Fiction. | LCGFT: Novels.

Classification: LCC PZ7.1.R4554 Dr 2023 (print) | LCC PZ7.1.R4554 (ebook) | DDC [Fic]—dc23

LC record available at https://lccn.loc.gov/2022053316

LC ebook record available at https://lccn.loc.gov/2022053317

For Luna—who is a very, very good dog

CONTENTS

CHAPTER ONE

Both Worlds

There is an old story about a seer. Every day the seer sits in a market square, predicting futures for the right price. One day, she's in the middle of a prediction when a friend runs up to her stall. Apparently, someone broke into the seer's house and stole all of her possessions. As the seer runs home, the other vendors in the square exchange grins. It's funny, they all think, that the seer could see the fates of others but not her own.

I was nine when Grammy first told me that story. I still remember walking with her, down by the very end of the greenway, listening to her voice as leaves trembled from their branches. Later, I read that story again in the appendix of the Cleary Family Guide Book. It's a famous tale because it is one of the most common fears in the seer community. We worry about balance. We wonder what will happen if we spend too much time looking at other people's futures. Will we forget to live our own precious lives? My solution: mix them up together in one big bowl.

That's why I'm hustling through the movie theater's parking lot, urging Jeffrey Johnson to hurry up. He might not know it, but we're heading to the location of my most recent vision.

"Aren't soccer players supposed to be fast?"

He's half scrolling on his phone as he tries to keep up with me.

"Didn't you tell me not to run through parking lots? You say that to me all the time. Like, more than my mom says it . . ."

I roll my eyes. He's right, though. Last year, I saved Jeffrey's life more times than I could count. And most of the incidents had to do with cars and parking lots. I have definitely given Jeffrey several stern speeches about his lack of awareness when surrounded by large, metal death traps. I guess it's a good sign that he's willing to take my advice, at least.

"You're right. I just don't want to miss the previews."

He slides his phone back in his pocket and frowns. "You don't even like the previews."

That's also true. And it's kind of flattering that he remembered such a small detail. I check the time on my phone, eye the line of people waiting out front, and lead Jeffrey around them, straight through the main doors.

"Hey. Wait. Don't we have to buy tickets?"

I wave my phone over one shoulder. "Already did."

He makes a noise of surprise, and I already know what he's going to say next. Not because I've seen this in a vision or anything, but just because I know Jeffrey. He has some very chivalrous concepts of what it means to go on a date. Even if we both technically got dropped off in his mom's minivan.

"You don't have to buy my ticket for this to be a date," I remind him. "If Sophie caught you thinking like that, she'd sit you down for a thirty-minute presentation."

He blushes a little. "So . . . this *is* a date?"

"Of course it is."

I glance over and catch the effect that has on him. He looks around like he's hoping that everyone within twenty feet of us has heard this very important announcement and knows we're on a date. We've mostly gone out with the whole group of friends, but Sophie and DeSean already had plans tonight. Jeffrey did take me to dinner once, alone, which would have probably counted as a real date if the waiter hadn't spent every possible second coming over to talk about how cute we looked. We barely got to talk to each other.

At some point this year, I did start thinking of Jeffrey as my boyfriend. And I'm pretty sure he thinks of me as his girl-friend? The only problem is that neither of us officially asked the other person out. Which is why if anyone in the world asked me if we were dating, I'd turn into a hermit crab and hide in my shell until the end of the universe.

Avery says we need to make things *official*. She's in ninth grade this year, which means she knows a whole new set of dating rules that we've never heard of before. But there's a big difference between knowing the rules and actually asking someone to be your boyfriend. Those two things are separated by a huge canyon of awkwardness that I haven't been brave enough to jump across yet.

"Celia?"

I look back. Jeffrey's standing behind the ropes with the ticket taker. I stare at him for a second in confusion. "What's wrong?"

"My ticket? You—you scanned yours but not mine . . ."

He trails off, like he's not sure if I actually bought him a ticket too. As if maybe this was one big miscommunication and he's going to have to go back outside and buy his own. I wave those concerns away with one hand and backtrack to where he's standing.

"Sorry. Just . . . a brain fart. Here."

Did I really just say the words *brain fart*? Reaching out, I scroll down to let the ticket taker scan the second ticket so that Jeffrey is free to slip past him. He has a little smile tugging at his lips.

"Brain fart, huh?"

I snort. "That's what Grammy always called them."

"She's so cool."

My heart skips a few beats as we walk past the concessions. He always talks about Grammy in the present tense, like she's still here with us. I want to feel like that's true. I'm always reading her advice in the guide book or hearing her voice in my head. But deep down, I know that she's gone.

"Popcorn?" Jeffrey asks.

"Maybe later. I want to get to our seats."

He frowns again. "Aren't they reserved?"

I shrug back at him. "Just in case."

Once again, Jeffrey is right. The seats *are* reserved. It's a new thing, getting to pick your seat ahead of time. Grammy would have hated it. Half of the fun—in her opinion—was trying to navigate through the seat savers and sprawling families to find the best seats still available. She always said it was one of her greatest talents. I feel that sharp pain as I think about the fact that we'll never walk up and down the aisles together again. It's like touching my tongue to a spot where a tooth used to be. Painful and sensitive and irreversible.

"I think we're in Theater Eleven," Jeffrey says. "It's over this way."

I smile and let him lead the way, even though I'm seeing this hallway for the fourth time this week. It looks exactly the same as it did in my visions. The lollipop-red carpets with random silver squiggles. Movie posters advertising coming attractions with bright colors or obnoxious explosions. I glance at my phone and know that in about twelve minutes, this hallway will be deserted. And that's when I need to come back to this spot.

Inside our theater, the house lights are still on. Commercials are playing as I follow Jeffrey up the stairs. He's counting the rows and looks like an explorer trying to navigate through ancient ruins to get us to the right seats. There's an older couple up in the back corner, and then a family down at the opposite end of our row. The rest of the place is pretty empty.

Which has me feeling nervous all over again.

Jeffrey and I have done a lot of hand holding. There's been smiling and laughing and big hugs. But if becoming official feels like an awkward leap, the idea of a first kiss seems even *more* awkward. Avery's tried to coach me on that subject as well—as our friend group's resident expert—but every time I think back through her advice, only three things come to mind:

1. Be careful about braces.
2. Eat a lot of mints/gum beforehand.
3. Don't keep your eyes open. That's super creepy.

I glance over to see if Jeffrey's as nervous as I am, but he's already plunked into his cushioned seat and he's messing with the controls of his recliner. I sit down and now there's just a pair of plush armrests between the two of us. The seats have us sitting so deep, though, that Jeffrey has to lean forward just so he can see me.

"Okay. So . . . do you remember everything that happened in the first movie?"

"Isn't this the one where the best friend turned out to be a robot?"

He groans. "No, no, no . . . That's a spinoff series. Okay. So in the first movie, we find out that there's a malfunction in the space-time continuum. And the entire crew ends up going . . ."

For about five minutes, Jeffrey explains one of the most complicated plots I've ever heard. It has me smiling, though. He's a really great storyteller. I've noticed this. The way he always wants to tell me about something that happened at soccer practice—or on his family's beach trip. And the more passionate he is on the subject, the more dramatic the story gets. It's one of my favorite things about him.

". . . and *that* is when they realize that they've actually arrived at their own home planet, but before *anyone* else occupied it. So . . . they're basically the settlers of their own future timeline!"

I nod enthusiastically when I realize he's done with his summary.

"Time travel. Got it."

He leans back in his seat, briefly vanishing into the massive puffs of leather. I laugh when he peeks back out. "This is a date . . . but you're totally *up to something*. Aren't you?"

I frown at him. "What?"

"You are!" He nods, confident in his guess now. "You're doing your . . ."

He waves all his fingers at me like he's performing a spell. The gesture always makes me laugh. One of the slight changes I made—based on Grammy's advice—was including my friends and the people I cared about in what I do. I didn't tell Jeffrey that I had used my gift to save *his* life specifically, but he knows I have an intuition about the future. The first thing he did when he found out was sit me down and ask me to tell him who'd win the next five Super Bowls. I had to explain that my gift didn't quite work that way, but he wasn't disappointed. More curious than anything.

I can tell Jeffrey and my friends are all slightly skeptical of what I mean when I say I can see the future. They just kind of assume I have good instincts or something. It's always hard for someone who doesn't have magic to fully believe that magic is real. Jeffrey has been more ready to accept the truth than the others. I waggle my fingers back at him.

"I'm pretty sure there aren't any spells that involve magic hands."

He laughs. "But I'm right. You're here for that."

"How'd you know?"

"Oh, there were *lots* of clues. You would be a horrible spy."

I pretend to be offended. "Oh yeah? Like what?"

"First, this theater is like ten minutes farther away than the one near our neighborhood on Pickard Road. And it's playing this exact same movie at this exact same time." He raises another finger as he counts off the clues that he's gathered. "Second, you've checked your phone like five times since we got here . . . but you haven't looked at your messages once. There are like eight unread texts. Which means you're keeping track of the time . . ."

I can't help grinning at that one. "Okay. That's pretty clever."

"And third," he says, clearly excited to add some icing to the cake, "I just told you a whole plot to the last movie—and inserted your name into the story twice, but you didn't even notice. Distracted! Which means you're doing your . . ."

He waggles his fingers again.

I laugh. "Fine. You caught me."

11

He does a little fist pump. "Knew it!"

"But for the record, I was distracted by *you* during the Wikipedia summary."

And those words have us both freezing like we were shot with stun rays from the movie we're about to watch. Jeffrey blushes. I realize that my words might mean more than they actually mean. I was just trying to say that, well, I was thinking about how much I liked him. But is the word *distracted* a code word for something else?

At that exact moment, the lights in the theater dim. There's shifting around us as people reach for snacks or drinks, preparing for the previews to start. I'm thankful for the dark because I know I'm probably blushing, too.

Jeffrey's still looking at me, obviously unsure if he should lean in closer or plunk back into the safety of his seat. My phone buzzes slightly and I realize it's time. I need to get downstairs.

"I'll be right back. I just have to save someone from making a *huge* mess in the lobby. I promise. Just this one thing, and then I'm all yours."

Those words act like a second hit from a stun-ray. Because saying *I'm all yours* feels like a line straight out of a bad romance novel. Jeffrey is blushing and I'm blushing and before it can get any more awkward, I duck down our row. I'm trying to focus on the real reason I came here tonight, but that last line keeps replaying in my head as I navigate the barely lit stairs.

Very smooth, Celia. Very smooth.

CHAPTER TWO

A Free Drink

The real reason we're here is my magic.

Since Grammy passed away, I've gotten nearly a dozen visions. It's taken a lot of practice to understand what I'm supposed to do. Last year, all my visions were of Jeffrey dying. Every time I would save him, another vision of another death would follow that one. Grammy eventually broke fate's grasp on him, sacrificing herself instead. I learned a lot then, and I've learned a lot since. It's been really helpful to know Grammy's theories about what kind of magic I have.

As I reach the hallway, I think about the letter she left

me. Grammy had two guesses about what kind of seer I am. In the history of our family, there have been dozens of different magical specializations. Every time a new type of magic occurred, it was recorded in the Cleary Family Guide Book. Some of my ancestors only had one focused gift. Others had a talent for multiple branches of magic. So far, both of Grammy's guesses about my powers have been right.

First, she called me a *Precognition Engineer*. The first word—*precognition*—really just means I see the future. The *engineer* part is where I'm a little different than my cousins or my older relatives. I feel like it makes me sound really official, like I went to college for magic or something. But all it really means is that I have the ability to move around my visions, investigating details, examining clues.

The other guess Grammy had was that I might be a *Proximity Clairvoyant.* I actually looked up *both* of those words in the dictionary after reading them in her note. *Clairvoyant* is another name for a seer, which makes me wonder why they didn't just use the word *seer* for all these different titles. The more important word is *proximity*. That means how close something is. And so far, my powers *only* work when someone is really close by. I've never had a vision of someone's future in Nepal or Australia. Not even down the road in our neighboring town of Buckden. Every single vision has been of someone that I'm actually close enough to help.

The hardest part has been figuring out what I should do to actually be helpful to people. It was easy with Jeffrey. He kept dying, so I kept saving him. Some of my recent visions don't offer anything quite that clear. In some of the visions, nothing even goes wrong. I've studied up as much as I can, but the family guide book keeps repeating the fact that I'll have to trust my gut. I've learned that even the smallest nudge can change someone's day, which can change their year, which can change their life. Tonight's case is a pretty easy one.

I glance down the hallway. There are brief bursts of sound from the nearest theater, vibrating with bass through the wall, but no one else is in the hallway. I aim for the side-door exit. Usually these are locked so that no one outside can come in. Everyone is supposed to enter through the main lobby to have their tickets checked first. These doors are only for people trying to leave the theater.

Except for the guy I saw in my dream. The same guy who is standing outside on the sidewalk right now. I know his name is Vincent because it's printed in small black-and-gold letters on the front of his shirt. He's peering through the glass doors, hoping someone notices him, as he tries to keep three bags of fast food and a tray of drinks secure in his arms. Right on cue, an older woman exits the bathroom. In my vision, she's the one who goes over to help him. But in this live version, I decide to intervene.

"Don't worry. I've got it."

She pauses mid-step, smiles at me, and heads back to her theater. Vincent, who is wearing an outfit that matches the rest of the movie theater's employees, heaves a huge sigh when I open the door for him.

"Hey, thanks so much," he says. "I've been out here for like five minutes. Flynn said he was going to let me back in. . . ."

In my vision, Vincent walks through the door at this point. Only it's usually the older woman who lets him in, and his elbow *always* snags on the strap of her purse. The motion catches him by surprise. He stumbles, dropping everything he's holding onto the floor. I have no idea why this moment mattered enough for me to get a glimpse of it, but I do know Vincent needs my help.

"No problem," I say. "It smells good."

He nods in agreement, adjusting to pass by me. That's when I see the slight twist in his new future. It helps that I've watched this accident four times. There might not be a purse strap for him to catch on, but my words are enough to distract him. His eyes are briefly on me, which means he doesn't see the snag in the carpet that his foot presses right up against.

I'm already moving—guided by my memory of the visions. With my foot still planted to keep the door open, I twist the upper half of my body. Away from the exit, back toward the theater hallway. Vincent stumbles and the drink tray flies out of his hands. Disaster is inevitable. But in the middle of my twist, I lean down slightly, and it's just enough to let me catch the tray before it crashes to the ground. Vincent steadies himself, securing the bags of food, and then stares in awe at the spot where he thought the drinks were about to spill.

"Wow. Close call." I carefully straighten. "Here are your drinks."

His eyes just keep getting wider.

"You caught that! Yo. That was *amazing*."

"It was a lucky catch," I say. "Here."

He takes the offered drinks, thanking me profusely. I watch him start down the hallway again, way more cautious this time, before he turns back around unexpectedly.

"Hey. Do you like orange drinks? Take that front one. On me."

"Oh. I'm fine. Really . . ."

"Trust me," he says. "You just saved my night. Take it. As a thank-you."

I imagine Jeffrey's reaction to me walking in with a soda from some random fast-food place. After a brief hesitation, I take the offered drink and thank Vincent.

"That's so nice! Have a good night!"

A thread of gold light flashes through the air. I was waiting for it. This is a very *new* thing for me, but I'm pretty sure it's a good sign. It feels like a confirmation that I did the right thing. It's almost like a special effect in a video game—when you finally find the secret door or use the right key. I know I'm the only one who can see the magical threads that hum in the air between the two of us. They hum and swirl until Vincent turns the corner. The golden light vanishes. I know I'll probably never see him again, but that sensation that I've helped him hangs in the air, almost like a chord of music that's just out of earshot. I have no idea what would have happened if he'd spilled the drinks. Maybe Vincent would have annoyed his friends. Or maybe he'd have been fired for making a big mess. Maybe nothing would have happened at all.

But the bright thread feels like a confirmation of what Grammy always taught me about being a seer. Our most sacred duty is to bring out a person's best possible future in this one wonderful life. I smile at that thought, take a quick sip of my newly earned soda, and head back into the movie. A final preview is playing. Jeffrey squints as I come down the row.

"Hey," I say. "Got this for you."

He inspects the cup and sees that the logo on the side doesn't match the movie theater.

"But . . . where did you get this from?"

I waggle my fingers at him and raise both eyebrows.

"Magic."

He smiles as I sink into my seat. I get a glimpse of the expression on his face. It's what I always loved about magic—especially about Grammy's magic. The ability to leave people wondering. That sort-of-lost but kind-of-found look that people would have on their faces after meeting with her for the first time. It feels nice to carry on that legacy.

It also feels nice when Jeffrey deliberately sets his newly gifted drink in the opposite cup holder. The movie's opening credits are starting when he sets his other hand slightly across both armrests, palm up and open in a clear invitation. I smile to myself and reach out, letting my fingers tangle with his. I briefly imagine Grammy leaning over and saying what she always used to say when we went to the movies. *This is the one with Brad Pitt, right?*

She'd say that before *every* movie. Even if it was a cartoon. My heart sinks suddenly in my chest, like a too-heavy anchor. I remember that, no matter what I do, Grammy will never sit down to watch another movie with me ever again. I swallow once, fighting back tears.

A little voice reminds me that this moment is just one of the many reasons Grammy sacrificed herself for me in the first place. She wanted me to live and have fun and hold hands and so much more. When I'm sure that I'm not going to cry, I snuggle back into my seat and adjust my grip on Jeffrey's hand.

It's just enough to let me forget, for a little while, about the gaping hole in my heart. I know it's still there, and I know it still hurts, but I can focus on the small victories of the evening instead. Vincent is out there having a far better night than he would have had without my help. Meanwhile, I have Jeffrey and I have my magic, and for now—that feels like more than enough.

CHAPTER THREE

Magic in the Courtyard

t's called *pivoting*."

Sophie shakes her head. "But you've got two thousand posts about sandwiches. You're the sandwich guy. I don't get how you can just stop posting about sandwiches. . . ."

"Because now I post about Slug," DeSean says. "It's brand pivoting. Any time you're moving to a new app, you can mix things up. Besides, people love Slug! I've had ten thousand new followers just this month."

Sophie's jaw nearly drops at that number. Earlier this year, DeSean bought a designer dog that might be one of the three most adorable creatures to walk the earth. It was hard enough for Sophie to accept the fact that DeSean had a legion of followers just for making sandwiches. He's literally famous in other countries for it. One of his recipes got featured on *Good Morning America*. Now she's having an even harder time understanding that Slug—a three-pound teacup pug—can really have more influence on social media than the rest of their school combined. She also wasn't super thrilled that DeSean bought a designer dog instead of a rescue. That argument lasted for pretty much the entire month of October.

We're out in the courtyard. It's been our place since sixth grade, and now it feels like it really is *our* place. Over the years, we've slowly moved from our corner table to the main table. The one that's always reserved for the eighth graders who choose this spot for lunch and have put in the most time. It's mostly our crew—DeSean, Sophie, Jeffrey, and me—but there are a few kids who crash with us every now and again. I can't help glancing over at the corner table where we started. There's a group of sixth graders there. I spy Nick Stone, our class president, passing out flyers for the upcoming winter dance. When school kicked off earlier this semester, they all kind of just ended up out here. Maybe they didn't know where else to go. But that led them to each other. I've watched over the past few months as they've formed their own friend group. People who weren't sure where they fit, until they realized how well they fit together. Like our crew did.

"If you say *pivot* again," Sophie threatens, "I'm going to stab you with this spork."

DeSean starts to protest but hesitates at the look on Sophie's face. We all spot Jeffrey making his way toward us, tiptoeing through the random groups while balancing his lunch tray.

"Hey, Jeffrey," DeSean calls. "What's it called in basketball? When a player keeps one foot on the ground, but turns around using the other foot . . ."

Jeffrey frowns as he takes his seat. "Pivoting."

Sophie growls at both of them. DeSean starts laughing hysterically. Jeffrey, as usual, looks slightly lost. "What?" he asks. "Not a basketball fan, Sophie? I was gonna see if anyone wanted to go to the game tonight. The last one was *wild*. We hit a half-court shot to win it at the buzzer. Tonight's game is getting so much hype."

Sophie shakes her head. "You lost me at basket . . . or ball . . . or buzzer. Or hype . . . I don't know. It was one of those words."

Jeffrey looks my way. "Want to come?"

"If I have to watch people sweat at each other, I prefer soccer."

He laughs. I can see how happy that comment makes him. The soccer team's season wrapped up a few weeks ago. I went to more athletic events in a month than I'd gone to in my entire life. Jeffrey was a captain this year. He started at center back, which meant he was always shouting things to the other players. It was kind of fun to see him like that. He's kind of shy most of the time but not out on the soccer field.

"What about you, DeSean?" he asks.

DeSean nods. "Sure. My sister can drive us."

"Oh. Right." Jeffrey looks a little embarrassed. "I meant to talk to you about that. Tatyana sent me a bill in the mail for the last time she drove us to a game. Remember? Back before break?"

"No way." DeSean scowls. "She said it was free."

"The bill looked very official. It had the JoyRide logo and everything. My mom was the one who opened it. She thought I'd signed up for some kind of crowdfunding app on my phone."

DeSean's already texting. "Tatyana . . . always trying to squeeze a dollar . . . Let me message . . ."

I can't help smiling. DeSean's big sister saved me a few times last year. I'm not sure how big Jeffrey's bill is for her car ride service, but I'd pay it myself if that wouldn't look suspicious. She's worth her weight in gold. Though I've told Jeffrey about my family's slightly different way of viewing the world, he has no idea that Grammy sacrificed herself for him. Which means he also has no idea that Tatyana helped save his life. Twice.

"She said that it was a 'clerical error,'" DeSean announces. "We're good for tonight."

Jeffrey glances at me and mouths the words *clerical*

error. I shrug back because I've never heard that term in my life. Sophie launches into another subject. I'm reaching for my lunch box when the scent of freshly baked cookies wafts into the air. I perk up a little because it's one of my favorite smells. But as I glance around the table, I realize no one packed cookies. Even if they had, I'm not sure how they'd get them to smell like they've just been pulled out of the oven.

That's so weird . . .

My stomach tightens uncomfortably when another scent reaches my nose, barely hidden beneath the first: a familiar campfire aroma. I'm starting to look nervously around the courtyard when it happens. I'm pulled away from my friends. A curtain of darkness. And then the expected vision arrives before me.

Except it's very *unexpected*.

I'm still in the courtyard. Just a few yards away from our table. My stomach jolts uncomfortably because I finally notice that I am still very much sitting at that table. I stare for a few seconds, not even breathing. Usually I can see everyone else. I can move around the vision at will. But this is the first time that I've ever seen . . . me. Is that future me? Present me? Some alternate-dimension version of me? It's hard not to notice that the scene matches *exactly* with what I was just experiencing. Jeffrey's there. Sophie and DeSean. The entire surroundings of the courtyard are identical to the previous moment.

"What is this?" I ask.

Those words unlock the vision. Without warning, my school-provided journal opens. All by itself. My eyes go wide. The other version of me also stares in disbelief. We both watch as the pages turn on their own. The journal cycles through before landing on a blank page. I've quietly moved closer, tiptoeing across the grass. It's like I'm afraid of scaring . . . myself.

Writing appears in the journal. Carefully drawn letters. Repeated over and over again. I see the name written free-hand. I see it in bubble letters and as an acrostic. It's written in thirty different colors. Random flowers appear on the page, the occasional flourish or heart. It spells out:

PATRICK

I'm trying to figure out what's happening when panic overcomes curiosity. My journal now has the name *Patrick* written inside it. Not once or twice. Dozens of times. Jeffrey's literally sitting right next to me. Without thinking, I reach out to slam the journal shut. The other Celia—the real me?—does the same thing at the exact same time. The journal closes and the vision snuffs out.

All the sound and color of the courtyard come rushing back to my senses. There's no longer a scent of cookies in the air. No hint of a campfire, either. Sophie, DeSean, and Jeffrey are all staring at me, though.

"Well?" Sophie asks impatiently. "What is it?"

I frown at her. "Huh?"

"You just slammed your hand down like a gavel. Usually that's followed by an announcement. Maybe a dissenting opinion. I don't know. Something. Pretty sure you just woke the dead with that sound."

I stare at my hand, then at the journal underneath it.

"Did any of you see that?"

Now they're all *really* watching me. This is my inner

circle. Three of the people who—besides family—know there's something different about being a Cleary. That doesn't stop them all from looking slightly concerned. It's easy to accept that I have an instinct about what's going to happen next. Not so easy to accept the idea that I'm seeing random things manifesting in the air that no one else can see. Besides, I'm not exactly eager to turn the page and fact-check this one in front of them. The name *Patrick* scribbled in my journal wouldn't be a fun discovery for Jeffrey, even if I'm dead certain none of them are written in my handwriting. It had to just be happening in my vision, though. There's no way words can appear in a journal out of thin air. . . .

"Sorry. There was a massive spider . . ." I pick up the journal, inspecting underneath it, and pretend to make a surprised face when I find nothing. "Must have missed it."

"Bold move," Jeffrey notes. "Going for the direct hand smash."

"My dad stepped on a spider one time," DeSean adds. "And *babies* came rushing out. It was legit something you'd see in a horror movie. Never seen him jump that high."

The conversation spins toward spiders and scary movies, and only Sophie keeps watching me closely. She raises an eyebrow and I give a subtle shake of the head that says: *Not now. We can talk later.* Because honestly, I need to figure out what actually happened before I can talk about it with anyone else. Step one: check to see if there's *actually* writing in my journal.

The bell rings ten minutes later. Sophie offers to come over tonight to study, and I know she really wants to know what's going on. I accept because I really do want to make an effort to keep my friends involved this time. No more flying solo.

Jeffrey walks me down to social studies. The whole time, the journal feels like it's burning a hole through my book bag. I'm embarrassed by even the possibility that I might be walking around with something that has some other boy's name written all over it, but that feeling slowly gives way to curiosity after Jeffrey ducks into his language arts class. I've never had a vision manifest like this one. For some reason, there were two scents? And the fact that I saw *myself* for the first time? It's all so strange, and Grammy taught me to ask questions about anything outside the norm. I've only ever seen *my* kinds of visions. A moment where I can explore and walk around and examine things that are happening to other people. What does it mean that the magic happened in a different way this time?

"And who on earth is Patrick?"

The minute bell rings. I take my seat in class, casually glance over one shoulder to make sure no one is watching, and flip to the page from my vision. *There's no way* . . . But my heart literally stops beating in my chest. Sure enough, there's an entire page full of scribbled versions of the name. *Patrick* with a heart. *Patrick* in red letters. *Patrick*s running left and right across the page. I put the journal safely back in my bag and smile to myself.

I've enjoyed a few quieter visions recently. The ones where I show up and give events a little nudge in the right direction. It was a nice change from last year with Jeffrey's repeating death visions. But this one has my spine tingling with excitement. This is something new. It's something I've been secretly hoping might happen.

Finally, a new challenge.

CHAPTER FOUR

Two Clues

The kitchen is empty when I get home.

One thing I've learned about losing someone you love is that you don't just lose them once. You lose them again and again. In quiet moments, where their noise or their presence once filled certain spaces. I used to come home and find Grammy in the middle of baking something. Or maybe she'd be sitting at the table, sipping a tea with a book on her lap. I can still picture her looking up at me as the door creaked open. Smiling as she dog-eared a page or burned some muffins, knowing it was the part of the day that we both looked forward to the most.

Those memories fade as I hear the sound of music thumping from Mom's room. Unnecessarily loud music. I sling my backpack onto the kitchen table and march upstairs. Mom's firm works from home two days a week now. It's been nice to have a slightly larger slice of her, but her taste in music is questionable at best. I glance through the open door. Mom's in the corner of her room, hunched over her Peloton, sprinting hard. A live voice is screaming at her:

"You are the change! You are the hill! You are the conqueror!"

I raise both eyebrows before waving. She sees the movement and motions for me to wait a second. There's one final pump coming. I can tell by how the music rises to an absurd level and the way Mom rises up slightly in her seat to pedal faster. The voice encourages her again:

"Hero mode! Dig deep! We're all climbing giants!"

A minute later, the music cuts off. There are directions

for a cooldown. Mom slides smoothly off the bike, wiping her face with a towel as she walks over.

"Climbing giants, huh?"

She grins. "I like that guy. Keeps me engaged. It's really been helping me focus in the middle of the day. Honestly, anything that gets me out of my chair and moving is a good thing."

I nod at that. "Well, you might want to turn down the music next time. Pretty sure you're going to be hearing from Mrs. Monroe next door. That was probably loud enough to knock all the figurines off her shelves."

Mom shakes her head. "Actually, Mrs. Monroe's the one who requested I turn it up. The speaker on her bike broke, but she still likes to do the organized rides. We text each other workout times and she listens in."

"You're telling me Mrs. Monroe is on the other side of that wall? And that she has also climbed giants?"

"Yes." Mom raises her voice. "Good workout, Emily!"

There's a loud whoop from our neighbor on the other side of the wall.

"Very normal," I say.

"Yeah? And since when did you care about normal?"

I grin at her. That's a Cleary question if there ever was one. Grammy used to say it to Mom, who always says it to me. It's the kind of thing we'll pass on in our family forever because really there's no such thing as normal in the Cleary ancestral line. Either you're a part of a magical generation like me, which means you see glimpses of the future, or you're like Mom, and you had to grow up with a parent who knew which night you were planning on sneaking out, no matter how well you'd planned it. Not much room for normal in either of those situations.

"Good point. I don't. Is it okay if Sophie comes over?"

Mom nods. "Of course. Just make sure homework gets done."

"It will. Thanks, Mom."

I turn around and I'm halfway to the stairs before she calls after me.

"Hey. How was school?" She lowers her voice slightly. "How's your magic going?"

Mom does this a *lot* now. Always checking in on me. She

knows Grammy usually did that after school. She also asks about my magic, but always by asking about something else first. It's always paired with a different question, like she's trying to make it feel normal. Mom knows that I used my powers to save Jeffrey, because Jeffrey wouldn't stop talking about my rescue of him at Jungle Rapids, and she eventually pieced two and two together. But she doesn't know that Grammy was *really* the one who saved him. She has no idea that Grammy died sacrificing herself for me. It's the one big secret I've kept from her. I still feel guilty for not telling her.

"School is good. Magic is good. I've got a good mystery going right now, actually."

"At school or with magic?"

"With magic," I say. "Something I haven't seen before. I'm going to have to do some digging in the Cleary Family Guide Book to figure it out."

Mom hesitates. "You are being safe, right? All the same rules apply, even when magic is involved. I hope you're not following prophecies into unmarked vans or anything."

I actually laugh out loud. I'm one hundred percent certain Mom would *not* approve of some of the missions I went on last year to save Jeffrey. Especially the time I hired Tatyana to drive me across town when I was supposed to be grounded. But her current fears are a little misplaced.

"Mom, I'm past the taking-candy-from-strangers-in-vans stage."

She strides forward and wraps an arm around me. "You have gotten taller. When did that happen?"

I stretch on my tiptoes. "Almost taller than you."

"Almost."

She plants a kiss on my cheek.

"Mom. You're sweating on me."

She plants another kiss.

"Only because I love you, dear."

It's a nice moment but brief, as another voice interrupts.

"Love you too, Celia!" Mrs. Monroe shouts through the wall. "Let me know if you ever want to come over and have some tea!"

We both hear the distant sound of a shower turning on. Mom and I stare at the wall for a second. She lowers her voice. "Hmm. Maybe we need to pad the walls. . . ."

That has both of us laughing.

I have about an hour to myself before Sophie arrives, but instead of rushing over to the Cleary Family Guide Book, I tackle chores first. Folding laundry and doing dishes. Mom taught me that sometimes the best way to solve a problem is to give it enough space that you can actually see it with proper perspective.

Sophie arrives just before dinnertime. Mom puts in an order for pizza as we both nestle into my room. Homework is a breeze—for once—and when everything's done, Sophie pulls her sandy-brown hair into a ponytail. This is her go-to move. It means she's shifting into business mode. Usually the ponytail leads to a long speech about whatever issue she's currently interested in. Apparently, this time I'm the issue that is up for discussion.

"Okay. Tell me what happened at lunch."

I pull out the notebook from my book bag. "Something weird."

"Weirder than normal?"

I turn the journal around so she can see the page. "Actually, yeah."

The massive gathering of scribbled *Patrick*s have Sophie squinting.

"It's not that weird. You like someone named Patrick."

"What? No! I like Jeffrey. This just . . . happened. While we were sitting there, my journal *opened* by itself. The writing just appeared. I slammed the book shut because I didn't want Jeffrey to see it. I don't even know anyone named Patrick."

"Yeah you do! Patrick Adams. He's in our language arts class."

I frown. "That's right. He's the really quiet kid. But . . . I haven't talked to him in . . . I don't even know. Like a year?"

"Okay . . ." Sophie considers the page. "Wait . . . This isn't even your handwriting."

"Exactly. Someone *else* wrote it. I just don't know why the name appeared in my journal. Or whose handwriting it is. Or . . . anything. I don't know anything."

Sophie raises one finger. "Research! How about you start with your little family book thingy and I'll start with our seventh-grade yearbook? We already have two clues."

"Two?" I echo. "The name *Patrick*. That's the first clue. What's the other one?"

"The hearts? The repetition? Clearly, whoever wrote these has a *huge* crush on him."

I can't believe I didn't think about that first. I was so worried about Jeffrey seeing the journal—and thinking I might really have a crush on someone else—that I didn't realize that this meant someone definitely has a crush on Patrick, whoever he is. Sophie's guess is a good one. This is the second clue, and there's no telling how long it would have taken me to figure it out. She offers me a determined nod, like she knows exactly how useful she's been, and I grin at her.

"Let's get to work."

Halfway through our research, the pepperoni pizza arrived. My primary focus is on the Cleary Family Guide Book while Sophie combs through old yearbooks.

". . . there's a spell here that provides '*clarity on the importance of the unknown*.'"

Sophie makes an interested noise. "Sounds promising."

I set down another piece of crust, trying to be careful not to get any grease on the book, although judging by the stain at the top of the current page, someone already spilled either tomato sauce or blood on it. Sophie's eyeing endless rows of pictures, patiently scanning the names in her search for other Patricks.

"Wow. Robin Van Noy's hair used to be red?"

I nod distractedly. "Yes. And hey! Focus!"

"Sorry. I just—wow. I really like that shade of red. It's almost like rosewood. She looks really cute . . ."

I nudge her with a foot and she makes a shooing gesture, continuing her search. I started my research in the section labeled *Anomalies*. I figured something as weird as a self-writing journal would be there, but it turns out that anomalies are reserved for the truly weird events. Seers who thought they'd witnessed other dimensions. A previous relative who claims that she turned her husband into a bowler hat. Reading just a few paragraphs in that section makes it clear I'm reading the wrong chapter. I need a little weird, not way the heck out there.

That led me to *Psychometry*—the branch of magic that focuses on visions that connect to specific items. It was actually Grammy's expertise, and I can see her notes lining every page. In fact, there's an entire paragraph about *water as an ideal but temporary conduit for magic*. The description has my mind spinning a little. As always, there's a comfort to seeing her familiar handwriting. But always followed by a wave of sadness. She expanded so much on this section in her lifetime, but even with her added information, I can't find anything about someone else's words *transferring* over to a journal unexpectedly.

"Hmm," I say, reading down the page. "Maybe this is like a summoning charm?"

"Summoning charm?" Sophie echoes. "Can you really do that? Summon something?"

I bite my lip, thinking. "Yeah. We summoned Jeffrey last year by accident."

"Like . . . through a portal?"

I laugh so hard that I almost drop my pizza on the bed. "No. He just showed up at our door. He was kind of dazed? So he kept saying really embarrassing stuff. Like how much he liked the freckles on my nose."

"That's super creepy," Sophie notes. "But they *are* cute freckles."

"Yeah, thanks."

"Wait! Got another one!" Sophie turns the yearbook around in triumph. "Patrick Connors! How'd we forget about him? He's a courtyard kid."

"When he's actually there," I reply. "I always just called him 'Connors.' Had no idea his name was Patrick. Didn't he set the record for most detentions in a single year?"

"Eighty-three," Sophie confirms. "It was kind of impressive. Anyways, that makes two . . ."

She taps the page again. I eye his picture. Patrick Connors has red hair, a freckled face, and the kind of sideways grin that literally translates to: *I'm up to something.* He's got sharp, hawkish features. I could definitely see someone thinking he's cute, but I have a hard time imagining someone having such a big crush on him that they'd write his name countless times in a journal.

"Can you flip back over to Patrick Adams?"

Sophie nods, thumbing through pages. "Here."

Even in his school picture, Patrick Adams looks *quiet*. Kind of like the photographer had to convince him to offer up even the beginning of a smile. He's Black and his hair—at least in this picture—was trimmed tight on both sides and left a little longer on top. He wears glasses and a collared shirt, and he looks like he's embarrassed that he was forced to make an appearance in the yearbook.

"He's cute," Sophie says. "A very *protect him at all costs* kind of cute."

"I remember when he did that presentation on the Outer Banks in fifth grade. Mrs. Harmon kept asking him to speak a little louder until Chloe Wu turned around and told her that we could hear him just fine and that she needed to stop interrupting him."

Sophie nods. "I remember that. She literally told a teacher to be quiet. Groundbreaking."

"But she did it *for* Patrick. We all kind of feel that way, right? He's one of those really sweet people that you feel like you'd beat someone up for. . . ." I make a note of that beside his name. "I still have to figure out if he's the *right* Patrick, though. Are they the only ones?"

"I've got a few more pages. Let me see."

We both patiently flip through our separate books. I find my eyes returning, again and again, to the suggested spell for *clarification*. It feels like my best bet, and it even has instructions for how to link that clarification to a specific item. There's a recipe listed with ingredients. I see Grammy's slight tweak to the spell in the margins: *Three zigzag stirs can reduce vertigo.*

"Nothing else," Sophie announces. "That's everyone."

"And you went through the sixth graders too?"

"Yes. Well. *These* sixth graders are now seventh graders. So, you'll need to get your hands on a list of the new class of sixth graders. Mrs. Schubert will have them."

"Got it. Come on, I need to make some tea. Want some?"

"Only if it will summon eight hours of sleep," Sophie says.

"My mom should be outside soon. Tell me how it works out, though. I'm really curious now."

I hand Sophie her math textbook, watching as she packs up.

"Hey. Thanks. It's . . . nice to have help. Without feeling weird."

"You *are* weird," Sophie replies. "So am I. This is what friends do. They help each other."

She bumps my shoulder as we head for the front door. Sophie waves goodbye to Mom, thanking her for the pizza. I stand there in the doorway as she gets in the car, smiling a little, because it really does feel like a breakthrough moment. Something worth celebrating. She helped me the same way she would have helped me do homework, or learn a new musical instrument. I never really imagined that I'd get to use my magic *and* be normal.

But that feeling only lasts as long as it takes for Sophie's mom to reach the end of the neighborhood. The second their taillights vanish, I grin wildly to myself. I'm not normal.

In fact, I'm about to go brew a potion to prove it.

Chapter Five

Symbolism Is Tricky

The steps of the spell are simple. As I set the kettle on the burner, I read back through just to make sure there aren't any weird side effects. The last thing I need is to randomly summon the Patrick in the journal to my door right before bedtime. That would lead to a *lot* of questions.

"... mix in two dollops of honey? How much is a dollop?"

I reach for the spice cabinet, adding the suggested teaspoons of cinnamon to the bottom of my mug. At least this concoction will taste good. Mom's watching a cooking show in the background, which makes my task slightly harder.

They're listing out ingredients to some kind of roast, so I make sure to read and reread each line just to be sure I've got the right amounts.

"...when the water starts to boil, fill your cup to the halfway mark. Immediately cover cup to trap the steam above the surface of the liquid..."

It takes me a second to find a Tupperware top that is a good fit for my mug. The tea kettle lets out a high-pitched whine. I pull it off and eye my mug like a proper scientist. I'm pretty sure Mr. Argyle would be proud, though he'd probably suggest wearing safety goggles next time.

"Okay. Halfway..."

The water pours out. Steam fills the air. As soon as I hit the halfway mark, I put the top on and press my hand down. The air around me is pleasantly warm now.

"What are you making?"

I nearly jump out of my skin. Mom's peeking over my shoulder.

"Mom. You scared me. It's tea."

"Magic tea?"

"Yes, magic tea."

"Hmm. Okay. Just don't set anything on fire. Or open any portals to other dimensions."

I shake my head and smile. "Can't make any promises."

My eyes trail through the paragraph one more time as Mom heads back over to the couch with a few snacks clutched in her arms. There are instructions for *binding* the item that needs clarification to my senses, but they're not super specific.

Once the clarifying potion has had time to brew, apply liberally to the item in question. This will form a link between the item and the imbiber. . . .

I'm assuming that I'm not supposed to just pour tea directly onto the journal. That seems like a good way to ruin the page entirely. I'm considering what to do when I spot Grammy's old paintbrushes, long dried on the kitchen windowsill. I reach out for them, but my hand pauses in midair. I can't finish the motion. A sadness wells up from deep inside my chest. A thrumming, unnamed feeling. It's so strong that it almost knocks me back a step. Grammy always loved to paint in her spare time. It was something she did to keep her mind calm. Something she'll never do again.

I have to physically shake myself. I shove those feelings down as deep as they'll go, and reach for the brushes. I snag the one with the largest tip. Removing the lid, I can see the steam gathered on the surface of the tea like fog. It looks cool. Like a mountain lake at dawn. Carefully I use the paintbrush to stir zigzags like Grammy's instructions said.

"Now . . . apply liberally . . ."

I open the journal to the page with all the Patricks. With quick strokes, I start to paint tea onto the page. It darkens everything. I can see little bits of cinnamon dotting the paper here and there. It takes some time, but I paint over every single repetition. It reminds me of a project I did in elementary school. Grammy even helped me with it. We had to make documents that looked like they'd been on an old ship. We used tea, but she also let me singe the edges with a candle. My final product looks a little like that. Old and weathered.

"Bottoms up," I say to no one.

The final step is to drink the rest of the tea. I set the journal on the kitchen table and start to sip. Mom's show plays in the background, a distant but pleasant buzz. The tea is still hot, so it takes a while for me to actually finish it. And then there's nothing to do but wait.

When successful, the potion will add clarification to an obscure topic or idea. The amount of clarity depends on the intensity of the brewed potion. It can also rely on the mental push given by the seer. . . .

"Hmm. Am I supposed to give a mental push? What is a mental push?"

I'm still debating what I should do when the words on the page shiver with movement. It's even creepier than what happened at lunch with the journal. That was like watching an invisible hand work on something. Almost like a time-lapse video. This feels less natural. It's more like watching reality *bend*. Each of the Patricks on the page starts to transform. At least, in my vision they do.

They look like stick-figure gymnasts, twisting this way and that, all on their own. Each name alters form, reshaping, until the word *Patrick* is no longer written anywhere in the journal at all. They've all taken on a new shape. The exact same shape each time. I reach down, rubbing a finger over the largest one. "What on earth . . ."

It takes a second to realize it looks like a symbol. The kind of thing you'd find on an ancient tomb or above the entrance to an abandoned ruin. Symbolism isn't exactly my strong suit. On a recent test, I had to name three symbols that could be found throughout the assigned book: *Hatchet* by Gary Paulsen. I earned very partial credit for remembering there was . . . a hatchet in the story. Which is literally the title of the book. Not my best work.

I'm still staring at the repeating emblems when the lines shiver again. Intuition tells me that the spell is about to end. I'm devoting each line to memory, focusing on the smallest details, when all of the Patricks wriggle back into existence. The journal returns back to normal. Well, kind of normal. I turn to a new page and start drawing the emblem from memory.

It's simple, almost elegant. I just wish I knew what it actually meant. Once my rough sketch is done, I take a picture with my phone. A quick scroll through contacts and I land on my cousin Mary. I text her the image.

It takes exactly five seconds for my phone to light up with a call. At first, I think that maybe Mary saw this moment coming. Maybe she was waiting for me or had sensed what would happen. But then I remember she's in college. College kids never go anywhere without their phones.

"Hey, Celia. What is that?"

"I was hoping you could tell me. It came up in one of my visions."

There are voices in the background. Mary says something; then the voices fade away. Now she sounds like she's moved to a stairwell or a bathroom. There's a slight echo.

"That looks like an emblem. Which falls under the category of Relic seers. Their visions literally look like this, but usually they're a lot more complicated. Imagine an entire *series* of emblems and images. They see them in order, and then they have to interpret the emblems to figure out what's going to happen in the future. I guess over the years, some of the emblems repeated enough that they started to figure out exactly what they meant. . . . Check page ninety-three."

I can't believe she remembers the actual page. I pull the Cleary Family Guide Book toward me and start flipping through it. I feel like I've read through most of the book, but I know absorbing all of the information in here would probably take a lifetime. There are so many notes and additions. I can't remember the section that Mary is talking about, though.

"Hmm," I say. "Ninety-three is all about 'Weather-Related Prophecies.'"

"Eighty-three!" Mary corrects herself. "Sorry. I'm a little tired."

"Yes, how dare you not remember this random page off the top of your head . . ."

I turn back. Sure enough, there's a chart. There are a *lot* of random charts throughout the book, but this is one of the more organized ones. Symbols and markings run down the far left column. Pretty much anything that Relic seers have encountered and interpreted over the years. I can't help wondering how far they date back. Are these the kind of markings you'd find at places like Stonehenge? I read quietly through the list before remembering Mary is on the phone.

"Sorry. I've got it. What do I do if this symbol isn't in the book?"

"I'm pretty sure you'd have to wait until the next Relic seer is born? They're the only ones who know how to interpret the symbols. And that could be . . . I don't know. A hundred years from now? Your best bet is if the symbol is already identified. . . ."

My eyes scan the page, skipping past emblems that don't match, until I finally spot it. There in the bottom corner. The two incomplete, conjoined circles. This particular symbol is listed under the category heading of "Woe and Warnings."

"Lovely . . ."

I find the coinciding page number and flip back to read the original reference. There—on page thirty-eight—I spy the first drawing of this symbol. There's an entire paragraph devoted to it. My stomach drops as I read. It isn't a positive paragraph. No sunshine or butterflies or lottery winners in this description. I skim through what's there:

This emblem is most commonly associated with collective danger. Not the fate of a single person, but rather the ill-fated future of a group of people. This group can be as large as the population of an entire country, or as small as an extended family. Either way, the emblem refers to . . .

My stomach drops to the floor. Mary is silent on the other end of the line.

"Doomsday," I finally say. "It's a doomsday scenario."

CHAPTER SIX

Coincidences

It's not easy to focus on Newton's laws when I've got a potential doomsday on my hands. As I sit in Mr. Argyle's class trying to take notes, little snippets from what I read in the Cleary Family Guide Book last night keep interrupting:

Doomsday scenarios don't necessarily mean the end of the world. More often, they simply represent a point of no return for the group that's involved. A sort of critical moment on the timeline that signals the end of something. Anything. Most people jump straight to meteors hitting the earth. More often, a doomsday will represent the loss of options. A sealing of fate, if you will . . .

". . . if you will?"

I glance up. The entire class is staring at me. Mr. Argyle's smiling in that way that all teachers smile when they're trying to be encouraging, but know you've totally blanked in the middle of class.

"Sorry? What?"

"We're out of good markers. Could you run next door and ask Mrs. Beasley for extras?"

I realize I'm in the back corner, seated closest to the door. The obvious person to ask.

"Sure. Should I take the hall pass?"

"It's right next door. You'll be fine." He turns back to the rest of the class. "Now, while we're waiting for Celia to return, I have been asked by the PTA to remind you that the big winter dance is coming up. I'm still not sure why we call it the winter dance if it's in November, but these flyers have all of the other information you need. . . ."

The door creaks slightly as I slip out into the hallway. It

gives me a second alone. A brief moment to clear my head and set things back on the proper mental shelves. I want to solve what's happening. I need to figure out the connection between Patrick and the doomsday symbol. And I need to figure out *which* Patrick the scenario is actually about. But I learned my lesson about keeping up with my classes. Mom will blame the magic if my grades slip the way they did last year.

After taking a deep breath, I knock on Mrs. Beasley's door. I can see flashes of movement through the little strip of glass. The handle turns and I'm about to ask for markers when I see who opened the door for me: it's Patrick Adams.

My mind goes completely blank. I forget about markers and class and everything. Only one fact exists, and my mouth spits that one thought out with an alarming lack of hesitation.

"Hey. You're Patrick Adams."

His eyebrows shoot up a little bit, like he's surprised that I know his name. The silence stretches and it is super awkward and everyone in his class is watching. Patrick turns back to Mrs. Beasley like she's the only lifeline that might save him from this much attention. I can't help wondering if this encounter is a sign? Is he the Patrick from the journal?

"Did you need something, Celia? Or did you come here to remind us of Patrick's name?"

I blush instantly. "Sorry. Mr. Argyle wanted to borrow some markers. Do you have any?"

She walks over to her whiteboard, inspecting the stray markers there. It takes me a second to realize that Patrick has *vanished*. Not by some act of magic or anything. He just used that brief moment when everyone's attention was on Mrs. Beasley to glide silently back to his seat. He's hunched down slightly, the neck of his hoodie half hiding his expression. But when we lock eyes, it's clear he's inspecting me. I imagine he's trying to figure out why I blurted his name out like that.

"Here you go."

Mrs. Beasley offers a hodgepodge collection of markers.

"Thanks!"

I take them, sneaking one more glance at Patrick before heading into the hallway. For some reason, my heart is pounding when the door closes behind me. What are the odds that I would get asked to go out in the hallway? And that he'd be the one to answer the door? I'm pretty sure Grammy used to say coincidences were bull's-eyes for a seer. The vision I had has to be connected to him. I'm trying to figure out what my next steps should be. Do I try to talk to him directly? Or just creepily trail him around school? I'm still lost in thought when movement catches my eye across the hall.

Patrick Connors emerges from the boy's bathroom.

"No way . . ."

Thankfully, he's too far away to hear me. His eyes dart left and right before he walks past the locker bay I'm standing in. I'm frozen in place, which I think is the only reason he doesn't spot me standing there, watching him. He aims for a classroom on the opposite end of the hallway.

What are the odds of running into *both* of them like this? Double coincidence.

As I turn back toward Mr. Argyle's class, I notice water running out of the boys' bathroom and into the hallway. I remember the look Patrick had on his face. How he looked like someone who was sneaking *away* from something. I shake my head. Always up to something. After a second, I head back into Mr. Argyle's room.

"Markers!" I say. "Oh. And there's water leaking out of the boys' bathroom."

Mr. Argyle rolls his eyes before heading over to the class phone to call it in. My classmates all start to whisper excitedly because water leaking from a toilet is possibly the best surprise the day will offer us. I'm still thinking about the odds of spotting both Patricks on the same day—less than a minute apart—when I haven't had a single thought about either of them all year.

All of this feels like it connects to the vision, to my magic.

I need to figure out what's happening, and fast.

But I've learned that when you want a day to go by fast, it goes by as slowly as possible. Science drags its feet. Even art class feels like it's slow-dancing with the clock. When the bell finally rings for lunch, it sounds like freedom, but then I remember I'll have three more periods until I'm able to go home and read through the guide book again.

Jeffrey, DeSean, and Sophie are already seated in the courtyard when I arrive. I plunk down, setting my lunch bag next to theirs. Jeffrey gives me a little nudge in greeting. I smile back at him. DeSean's in the middle of an excited rant that has Sophie sighing with boredom.

"Seriously. You should have been there."

Jeffrey nods. "You both missed out on a legendary game."

"You mean last night?" I ask.

"Totally," DeSean says, and I'm not sure I've ever seen him quite so animated. "We were down two with literally one second left on the clock—"

Jeffrey cuts in. "That's not even enough time to catch the ball usually!"

"But he catches it and slings it . . . one-handed!"

"Nothing but net," Jeffrey finishes. "The crowd went wild. We all ran onto the court. That's *two* full-court shots—in back-to-back games. It was amazing."

"And he was super cool about it," DeSean adds. "He just let everyone swarm around him. Like he expected to make it or something. Patrick is the coolest."

Sophie had a complaint about sports on the tip of her tongue, but that final sentence has her jaw hanging slightly open. I'm sure I have the same look. We catch each other's eye. I haven't even told her about my run-ins with the Patricks today. What are the odds that Jeffrey and DeSean would bring one of them up? I frown, though, because I'm having a hard time imagining either Patrick hitting a game-winning shot in a basketball game. I can't resist asking the most obvious question.

"Which one? Adams or Connors?"

Jeffrey frowns. "What?"

"Was it Patrick Adams or Patrick Connors?"

"Oh. Neither. It was Patrick Bell."

"Kid is the *coolest*," DeSean repeats.

An alarm is going off in my head. Sophie's looking like she's thinking the same thing.

There's a third Patrick.

CHAPTER SEVEN

Little Lies

"Why aren't we catching the bus?" Jeffrey asks, trying to keep up with me as I whip through the hallways, aiming for the library.

"I need to do some research. For my . . ."

I waggle my fingers at him. His eyes light up a little. I want to let Jeffrey into this part of my life, but I don't want to let him *so far* in that he connects the dots of what happened to him last year—and why I suddenly came crashing into his life. The two of us barely dodge a teacher who's exiting her room with a media cart.

"They have books in the library about that?" Jeffrey asks.

"Kind of. Come on."

Our librarian is Mrs. Schubert. I spy her roaming the shelves at the back of the room, plucking new books to set out on display. I've always liked her. Today she's wearing her red hair in a braid that runs over one shoulder. Her purple-rimmed glasses match her purple cardigan. I know she's not a seer or anything like that, but it's almost magical how often she's picked out the right book for me to read over the years. She spots us near the reference desk and offers a wave.

"Need some help?"

"I'm doing a project for statistics. Mr. Argyle wanted me to calculate the ten most common names in our school. Do you have a list like that?"

Mrs. Schubert is the yearbook teacher too, so I know she's got class rosters. I need to look at those lists if I'm going to get a firm grasp on what to do next about the Patrick dilemma. The only problem is that I'm lying—to a teacher—and I'm doing it in front of Jeffrey. Both of them frown at me for different reasons.

"I have the list the yearbook club uses," Mrs. Schubert answers. "But I can't let you take it home. You'll have to do the work here in the library. Will you have enough time, or do you want to come back tomorrow during lunch?"

"Now would be great!"

She heads off into her cozy little office to find it. Jeffrey's still frowning because he's in Argyle's math class with me, and he knows there's no project assigned. We're not even studying statistics right now. He lowers his voice to a whisper.

"You just lied to Mrs. Schubert."

I've been thinking about this ever since lunch. Last year, I did have to do a lot of sneaking around. Little lies that didn't hurt anyone—and each one helped me save Jeffrey. Grammy tried to steer me away from those kinds of tactics last year. She thought it was a slippery slope to make those lies a core part of how I use my magic. I've been trying to take that advice to heart, but sometimes there are exceptions to the rules, ways to bend but not break them.

"Actually, Mr. Argyle said we could do an extra-credit project. Remember?"

He frowns again. "But we're in the middle of a geometry unit."

"For now," I say. "The next unit on the syllabus is statistics. I'll turn this in then."

"Okay, but what's the *real* reason you want the list?"

I let out a sigh. I was hoping to avoid this part. "I'll show you."

Mrs. Schubert comes back with a packet of papers that have seen better days. There are scribbled notes up and down the margins—which briefly reminds me of the Cleary Family Guide Book. All of these notes, however, coordinate to pages in the yearbook.

"That list doesn't leave the library," Mrs. Schubert reminds us. "Need anything else?"

When we shake our heads, she roams back to the book display she was working on. Jeffrey follows me to a corner table, and I set the list and my notebook out side by side. I have to take a deep breath before turning to the most incriminating page in my notebook.

There are *Patrick*s scattered everywhere. Jeffrey's eyes widen as he takes it all in. I know he's jumping to all the wrong conclusions. I've got an explanation ready, but I've seen this kind of thing happen with other dating relationships at our school. One wrong move—one misunderstanding—can ruin everything. His expression shifts from surprised to upset. I can see his entire body start to lean away. It's like he wants nothing more than to grab his book bag and leave. I'm about to start my explanation when he blinks. His face breaks into an unexpected smile.

"Whose journal is this?" he asks.

"It's mine."

He frowns. "But that's not your handwriting."

There's a tug in my chest. I want to throw both arms around him. I could almost kiss him, if it wouldn't be super embarrassing to have a first kiss in a library. He knows *my* handwriting.

"So you're not mad?"

"No. Well. I mean, I was for like . . . two seconds. Because it would be super awkward if you were writing someone else's name in your journal. But . . . who wrote that?"

"That's what I'm trying to figure out. These appeared in

my journal at lunch yesterday. It's connected to my visions. There's something big that's happening with someone at our school named Patrick. I thought there were just two of them. And then I found out from you today that there's a third Patrick. I have to make sure there aren't any more. I needed the sixth-grade list—and I need to double-check anyone who transferred. I have to make sure I have all of the information, or I might end up trying to help the wrong Patrick."

"Why?" Jeffrey asks. "What's going to happen to them?"

"That's the problem," I say. "I don't know. We have to cross this bridge first."

And my heart thrums again because Jeffrey reaches for one of the lists and immediately starts scanning. Just like with Sophie, it's kind of cool to have someone who trusts me, even if they don't fully understand how my mind or my powers work. We both dive in. Jeffrey has the sixth graders. I start with the seventh-grade list but don't find a single Patrick in the group. As soon as I switch over to eighth grade, though, the names I already know stand out like beacons on the page.

Patrick Adams comes first. Followed by Patrick Bell—who must have transferred from another school because he wasn't in the yearbook when Sophie and I searched last night. On the top of the next page, Patrick Connors's name gleams. My eyes scan the list carefully while Jeffrey hums a little song to himself. It takes us about ten minutes, but we finish our lists and don't find another Patrick. Just to be sure, we trade pages and start scanning again. The result is the same.

"Only three of them?"

"Three," he confirms. "Adams, Bell, Connors. ABC."

"That's convenient. Okay. I need to get home. . . ."

But Jeffrey shakes his head. "You told Mrs. Schubert we're doing a project. We can't lie to her. Which means we need to actually do the 'common names' project. You can turn it in during the next unit. Thirty more minutes. Come on. I'll help."

Every part of me wants to rush home and get to the bottom of the bigger mystery, but I can imagine Grammy off to the side, smiling mischievously at Jeffrey's suggestion. I know she did what she did to save me, but I can imagine her thinking of Jeffrey's influence on me as a fine side effect.

"Fine. Thirty minutes."

He smiles and starts humming that song again. We work through the lists, focusing on my made-up task, and start by trying to pinpoint the most obvious names. *Lily* emerges as contender for the most popular girls' name. It's in a tight competition, though, with *Mason* and *Liam* on the boys' side. We narrow our list down to the most common ten names before the thirty minutes are up. Mrs. Schubert sweeps over to collect the list, promising to keep it on hand for the next time we visit to finish the project.

All the other names—the *John*s and *Olivia*s and *Arlo*s—are dancing around and mixing together in my brain. But one name sits at the front of my mind, highlighted in bold: *Patrick.* I've finally taken a clear step forward. It feels like progress. I know the three Patricks who could potentially be involved. Coincidentally, all three of them came up today in the exact same thirty-minute window of time. I think the Cleary Family Guide Book would say that's more than a coincidence—it's fate.

As we leave the library, Jeffrey asks, "What will you do next?"

"I have my list. Now I just need to learn more about each of them."

"So . . . you'll follow them? Like a detective?"

The suggestion sets off a light bulb of an idea. I've been trying to figure out how to find out more about each of them without being creepy. Of course. I can *follow* them.

"Not literally," I say out loud. "I can follow them on social media."

"Smart," he says. "Except, you know, the fact that you don't have any social media accounts . . ."

"True. I'll need help from an expert."

Jeffrey shrugs. "I mean, if you need my help . . ."

The silence stretches awkwardly between us. He's watching me and waiting for me to confirm that he is, in fact, the expert that I was referring to.

"Uhh . . . yeah . . . I'm not sure reposting soccer videos makes you a social media expert."

He snorts. "Hey. I do a lot of editing on those. They're really cool videos."

"I'm sure they are, but I had someone else in mind. . . ."

He thinks for a second. "DeSean?"

"DeSean is an influencer. If I wanted to build my brand as a seer, he'd be perfect. What I really need is someone who knows how to *find* people on social media. . . ."

"Like . . . a stalker?"

"Researcher!" I correct. "Come on. Who knows everything about *every* kind of social media?"

"Oh! Avery!"

I nod. Avery has spent four months in ninth grade, and already seems to know more than the rest of our crew combined. Finding out things on social media is her area of expertise. I pull my phone out and text her.

"I'm sorry," I say to Jeffrey. "You can be my backup social media advisor."

He shrugs. "I'm honestly just glad you don't have a crush on someone named Patrick."

Our shoulders bump together as we walk. We both smile

to ourselves. I'm not the type of person to scribble names with hearts in a journal, but we're smiling because we both know whose name we would write. We head for the carpool lane. For the first time in the last few days, I'm able to set the name *Patrick* off to the side on a shelf in my mind. My stomach flutters nervously as I think about the name that replaces it. The name of the boy walking beside me.

I just might have a big crush on Jeffrey Johnson.

CHAPTER EIGHT

Social Media Orientation

Avery knocks on our front door while Mom's bustling around, getting ready for a date tonight. Mom's gone on dates since I was little, but leaving me at home by myself? That part is new. Grammy would always be there to keep an eye on the townhome whenever Mom went out with friends after work or got dinner with someone. It's new to be trusted like this, though it's a status that comes with plenty of warnings.

"Jeffrey's not coming over, correct?" Mom asks as she jams her right foot into a shoe that doesn't look nearly big enough. "Oh! Hey, Avery! Good to see you."

Avery waves. "Hey, Mrs. C!"

I toss my mom the coat she's searching for.

"It's just me and Avery, Mom. Promise."

"Okay. Nothing against Jeffrey. He's a nice boy. Just . . . you know . . ."

Avery smirks at me, like she knows, but I've never even kissed Jeffrey. So I'm not really sure what Mom thinks would happen. The most likely outcome is that we'd binge-watch four episodes of the latest season of *Lost in Orange County*. Jeffrey pretends he doesn't like it, but I caught him reading a catch-up summary of the first season last week. I'm pretty sure he's in deeper than me.

"Dinner's in the fridge. Just make sure to turn the oven off after you heat it up."

She pauses in front of the mirror. Her hair's in a tight braid like mine. Sometimes I forget how much we look alike. I have her wheat-colored eyebrows. A scattershot of freckles runs across the bridges of both our noses. They look like the kind that artists would paint on a doll. The only slight dif-ference is that I'm already as tall as her—with Grammy's long-limbed height. Other than that, we're clear-cut copies of each other.

"You look hot, Mrs. C!" Avery says. "I like the jacket."

It's a chic leather one. And she's right. Mom looks good.

"Have fun on your date, Mom. Don't worry about us."

"I'll be home around eight. Love you, girls."

We both watch her head for the front door. Her footsteps echo, then a groan from the bottom step on the porch and the slam of a car door. Avery turns around and all but explodes with excitement.

"Please tell me your text was real."

"Very real."

She waves her phone. "Amazing. Okay. Let's make your FlyBy profile first. . . ."

Before Avery came over, I looked up what I could find in the Cleary Family Guide Book. Apparently, any spying done by a seer has a very specific and uncreative name: *scrying*. The guide book makes it clear that this is the favorite investigative tool of seers. There are warnings, of course. The creepiest one was: *Be careful of using such mediums to look* out at the wider world. *You never know what might be look-ing back.* Even thinking about that line still gives me goose bumps.

It also had me deciding to use the lowest-level potion I could find. Most of the old-school definitions required some-thing from the person you wanted to scry on. One paragraph mentioned securing a lock of hair or even a toenail (gross). Another mentioned creating a life-size statue or commis-sioning an oil painting (expensive). I wasn't sure how to do *any* of that, but it did give me an idea for a different strategy. My hope is to combine Avery's expertise with a new version of the magic.

"How many social media apps are there?"

Avery plunks down on the couch. "Tons, but let's start with the basics. . . ."

It takes about thirty minutes to go through my orienta-tion on the classics, from Instagram to TikTok, and every-thing in between. Avery focuses the most on what's popular now, though: FlyBy. She says it has most of the same fea-tures as the older platforms, but FlyBy is all about being the best *commenter*. Who's the person who can reply with the funniest video? It's that person who ends up becoming famous—rather than the original poster.

Avery gives me a list of people I *just have to follow*. Some are from the high school, but some of them are my class-mates. There's John Michael Lewis—a seventh grader—who responds with videos of himself folding up his quizzes in unique, funny ways before turning them in. It's actually kind of genius.

From there, she helps me set up an Instagram account and even signs me up on something called 37 Seconds. I'm surprised this one is popular, but Avery says it's her favorite. Apparently, it's legal to film a person for exactly thirty-seven seconds. Any more than that and it requires their signed permission. The app has been capturing thirty-seven-second snippets of people for almost five years, and it plays them randomly out into the world. She shows me a few examples, but they're all bizarrely normal. A guy mow-ing his lawn. Someone trying to return a pair of shoes to a department store.

"This is so weird. . . ."

"It's amazing," Avery says. "All right. You said you had *specific* people you wanted to follow?"

"Yes. This is going to sound weird, but I need to find accounts for Patrick Adams, Patrick Bell, and Patrick Connors. . . ."

Avery nods slowly. "You're right. That does sound weird. The search bar is in the corner. Why don't you start with Instagram, and I'll start with FlyBy?"

Our search begins. I note the fact that this particular prophecy has already involved way more research than anything else I've had to do so far. Usually I just see a moment in the future and plan a way to intervene or help. Grammy never told me math *and* social media stalking would be involved. I'm still typing in Patrick Adams's name when Avery wags her phone in the air.

"Found Patrick Connors . . . He's got a pretty active FlyBy account. . . ."

Typing in *Patrick Adams* results in hundreds of profiles. I scroll down slowly, looking for a thumbnail that even remotely resembles him. A few of them feature cartoon characters. I click those, but none of the pictures or locations seem like a fit for the one I know from class.

Avery is way faster than me. "I'll send you that profile . . . Now let me find Patrick Bell. . . ."

I'm still scanning my first set of names when she pumps a celebratory fist.

"Got him. Whoa. He's got a *lot* of views on his most recent video. And . . . whoa! Lady Cloud commented on it! She's one of the top five FlyBy accounts. . . ."

Avery turns the screen so we can both see. I lean a little closer and watch the scene unfold. A basketball court. Loud cheering. I'm about to ask which one is Patrick Bell when I remember what DeSean and Jeffrey said at lunch. He's the one who hits a game-winning shot.

The ball gets passed to a boy with tan skin and light brown hair. We both watch him heave the basketball to the opposite end of the court. It doesn't look like he's thrown it nearly hard enough, but the ball soars unnaturally through the air. There's a halting moment where everyone—the players and the coaches and the crowd—all stop to watch. And then it drops right into the basket. An impossible shot.

Patrick Bell turns around and shrugs, like that was the most normal thing that could have happened. The crowd mobs him and the video restarts. Avery's right. A number in the corner shows it's been watched nearly one hundred thousand times already.

"He's really cute," Avery notes. "But I don't remember him at all."

"I'm pretty sure he transferred. Are there other videos?"

She taps on his account, scrolling down. We see *another* game-winning shot from the game earlier this week. I'd forgotten about that. He's scored *two* lucky shots in back-to-back games. There are a few other random videos, and then I spot one where he's talking directly to the camera.

"That one. What's he saying?"

Avery has to tap her phone screen to get the sound on. Patrick's voice pours out.

". . . and your boy? *Starting* tonight. Finally! Catch us at six p.m.! We're in the side gym!"

She keeps scrolling to other videos. Almost everything is basketball related. Practice drills where he's dribbling two balls at once while looking at the camera. Videos of his teammates goofing off before practices. His family took a beach trip earlier in the fall and there are a few videos of him skimboarding. But clearly, basketball is the centerpiece of his life.

"What's that hashtag mean?" I point to the corner of the screen. "I keep seeing it on the earlier posts. What is the Sixth Man?"

Avery swipes over to a search engine and types the phrase in. She reads the info that pops up. "*The Sixth Man Award goes to the best player who is not a starter. It is called the "Sixth Man" because there are traditionally five starting players for a team in basketball. . . .*'"

"Interesting," I say, thinking out loud. "That means he was sitting on the bench to start the season? And then he had that video where he announced he was in the starting lineup. That's a big deal, isn't it? Who starts and who doesn't? And then he hit two game-winning shots?"

Avery nods. "Must be practicing a lot. I mean, there were all those training videos."

"It's pretty lucky, too. It's not like you can count on making full-court shots." I pull out my journal and start taking notes. "Can you pull up the video of Patrick Connors?"

I'm amazed how fast she whips from one profile to the next. In less than a breath, we're staring at the profile she found for Patrick Connors. His favorite hobbies are also very clear. The same backdrop is featured in most of the videos. It's the skate park near downtown. Avery and I used to go there after school sometimes. She cycles through videos of him trying various tricks.

"All right. He's into skateboarding. . . ." I take more notes in my journal.

Avery nods. "He's not bad, either. Good board control."

"Do you miss skating?"

"Sometimes," she answers. "I'm kind of scared to go back, I guess? I just . . . stopped going. Back when . . . well, you know . . ."

She's right. I do know. Back when she abandoned us.

During our big fight. She started focusing so much on cheerleading—and becoming a part of that crowd—that she abandoned both the Courtyard Kids *and* all the after-school skate park crews. I nudge her shoulder with mine.

"You act like they wouldn't want you back. I wanted you back."

She sighs. "Yeah. I know I'll be really rusty, too. Patrick is doing things that I *used* to be able to do. Maybe you're right. Maybe I should go one day after school . . . anyways. We've got these two, but I can't find an account for Patrick Adams. I just searched Instagram, too, and there's nothing. . . ."

"Are there any other apps he might be on?"

"Hmm. If he's old-school, he might be on YouTube. . . ."

I pull out my own phone and accept the two profile invitations that Avery has sent me. I scroll through and favorite the videos that I think will be the most useful based on the description of the scrying spell in the book. Once I've got those saved, I go back to Patrick Connors's page. There isn't any video evidence of whatever he did in the bathroom earlier today. I do notice that he posts a video pretty much at the same time every day, but for some reason, there's no content today.

That's interesting.

"Is this him?"

Avery's question draws my attention. She's holding out her phone. Sure enough, there's Patrick Adams, taking up half the screen. The other half has a bubbled font that makes no sense. I literally have to read it out loud for my brain to process it.

"*How to Start Your New Leaf Blower?*"

Avery hits play. "It's an instructional video. The whole channel is instructional videos."

I lean in curiously. I've never seen anything like this, but I feel like it's what Mom always watches when we get a new accessory in the house. Patrick Adams seems exactly how I've always known him. His voice is relatively quiet. He's shy and reserved. The only slice of bravery—and it's a pretty large slice—is the fact that he made these videos in the first place. He carefully walks through each step, explains which buttons to press, and before long he's got his own leaf blower's engine gunning. He demonstrates blowing a pile of leaves before turning and offering a thumbs-up to the camera. It cuts away to a list reminding people of the steps to follow.

"And all of the videos are like this?"

Avery scrolls. "Pretty much."

There's a tutorial for a homemade altimeter, a video about lawn mower settings, and an entire series on building your own cleaning robot. There aren't thousands of views, but the comments are all from people thanking Patrick profusely for helping them. Avery points out that he's gone through and replied to each of them, saying it was his pleasure. I realize that he didn't make the videos to gain a big following, like most of our classmates would. He made these videos because he actually wanted to help people.

"I had a computer class with him," Avery says. "He never said a word."

"He's really shy. I didn't even know what his voice sounded like until we watched these."

"Well, you've got the accounts," Avery announces. "And your weird notes on each of them. Want to tell me why we're researching all the Patricks at your school? That seems very specific."

I've already told Jeffrey and Sophie. It feels strange to let so many people in when I spent so much time last year trying to hide what I could do. It's not lost on me either that Avery was the reason I tried to hide who I was in the first place. My family's magic is what broke up our friendship. I have to believe that's all behind us now. I clear my throat and dive right in.

"One of them is involved in a doomsday prophecy."

Avery's eyes go wide. "You mean like . . . Ice Age, end of the world–type stuff?"

"I'm not sure yet. Next step: scrying."

CHAPTER NINE

Scrying in the Modern Age

I was kind of hoping Avery would head home before I attempted the magic. It's always weird to have someone watching you perform a spell. Most of the time, only I can see what's happening. I imagine it's a lot like watching someone play video games, but not being able to see the screen. Just the way they're pushing the buttons on the controller. That would be super awkward.

Avery insists on staying, though. For some reason, this means more to me than all of the others. Sophie and Jeffrey and Mom: they've always supported me. But Avery and I had a fight *because* of magic. The fact that she's willing to jump in now? It's a sign of just how far we've come.

I'm reading back through the description of the scrying spell when Avery returns to the kitchen. I glance up and do a double take. "Why are you wearing a helmet?"

She's got my old bike helmet strapped on. There's a peeling sunflower sticker on the front.

"I don't know?" she says, half laughing. "Isn't it dangerous? What if random items start floating through the air or something?"

I grin at her. "You watch too much TV."

"You don't watch enough TV," she throws back. "What do we do?"

"The spell says that I need to '*attempt to unite body and mind with singular focus. Once they are synchronized, consume the spell's ingredients and direct your focus on the item in question. . . .*' How do I do that? Unite my body and my mind . . ."

Avery frowns. "Yoga?"

"Hmm. That's not a bad idea. But every time we did yoga

in gym class, I felt like I was the opposite of focused. It was usually the most distracting part of the warm-up. . . ."

"That's just because Wes Bearden always breathed so heavily."

"True," I say, thinking. "Wait. Wait, I've got it. Come on."

Avery grabs our phones. I snag the Cleary Family Guide Book and the prepared cup of tea. We head up the stairs and into my mom's room. She's never cared too much about privacy. We go in and out of each other's rooms all the time. I flip the light switch, make sure it's not too messy, and then lead Avery to Mom's Peloton bike.

"Body and mind," I say, climbing onto the bike. "I'm pretty sure there's a silent mode. . . ."

As I start to pedal, the screen hums to life. I click through options and the audio goes mute. I turn the screen's color down until it goes completely blank. There's a small ledge that's perfect for my phone. Avery sets it there in front of me as I pick up speed. She hovers at the back of the room. I think she's going to be a distraction, but after a minute, I've got a rhythm. My mind is focused. I reach out my left hand.

Avery brings my tea forward. It takes a small adjustment to keep pedaling without spilling it all over the floor. *Consume the spell's ingredients and direct your focus on the item in question.* Carefully I begin sipping. The recipe wasn't overly complex—but the taste is an absolute disaster. Like sipping tire tracks. I fight against gagging and keep gulping it down. I can feel a slight tightening in my skull. My eyes water a little, but I force myself to keep drinking. When the cup's empty, I reach out again. Avery sweeps in to take the cup away. I hit play on the first saved video: Patrick Connors. It starts to play as I lean forward, picking up speed like I'm in a race.

Nothing happens. At first.

The video loops back to the start. Patrick Connors flips his board, lands, and pumps a fist at the camera. I watch him skate off before the video loops a third time. I'm wondering if maybe I didn't make enough tea when the screen *flickers*. Light fills my vision. The screen *underneath* my phone colors to life. On the actual Peloton. Instead of a program instructor, though, it's another video of Patrick Connors. I scramble to lift my own phone out of the way. I have to tap the volume button to get it to turn up a bit. It seems impossible, but I'm watching extra footage of Patrick Connors.

This has to be the scrying vision.

He's in the same skate park. I watch from a slightly different angle as he attempts a new trick. Another kid comes in from off-screen. The timing is so unlucky. The very back of his board catches Patrick's board at just the wrong moment. I can see it on his face when he figures out he's about to absolutely bust it. And he does the one thing you *don't* do. He shoves out his hands to brace for impact. People say you're supposed to just take the blow with your body. Let the impact spread across far sturdier body parts. But all of the force of his fall catches on his right wrist, and I can't help wincing because I can all but hear the bone snap.

The vision flickers again. Patrick Connors is at a doctor's office. His mom—at least I assume it's his mom—is shaking her head as the doctor reveals two hairline fractures. They start getting the cast ready. And then the screen goes blank.

I come gasping back to the present. My feet have stopped pedaling.

"Did it work?" Avery asks from somewhere behind me.

I start to pick up my speed again. "You couldn't see that?"

"See what? You were just pedaling . . ."

Interesting. The vision appeared on the Peloton screen but only for me. I guess that makes sense. I'm the one with the magic. "I saw a glimpse of Patrick Connors. He broke his wrist at the skate park. That's probably why he didn't post a video today. . . . Now, for the next one . . ."

Reaching out, I swipe over to the video of Patrick Adams that's saved on my phone. He's pressing a small button on his orange-and-white leaf blower when I reach the same speed as before, as I find the same rhythm. The scrying spell starts again.

A new video appears on the Peloton screen. I slide my phone to the side and watch as Patrick Adams appears. He's standing stock-still, perfect posture, waiting for someone. I have a decent angle of the entire room. There's a long table in front of him and a few other kids our age. Judges are circling around the central area, making notes. It looks like some kind of science fair.

But another glance shows that it's all *robotics*. Little gadgets and machines. I increase the volume and can just barely hear the buzz of little engines and gears. He's in some kind of robotics competition? One of the judges stops at his table and gestures. Patrick Adams looks ready. He picks up his remote. The machine looks like one of those Roomba cleaners, but I watch as Patrick makes the machine lift itself up an inch at a time. There are two stilts—which I'm sure is *not* the scientific term—on each side of the device. I'm not sure what the point of his invention is until I see the label on his display: *The Staircase Cleaner.*

The judge scribbles down a few notes. We watch the device lift up in the perfect motion to climb a single step. Patrick is smiling to himself, satisfied with his work, when a small *explosion* sounds. Smoke fills the air. No one's hurt, but everyone turns to look as helpers come in with an extinguisher to keep the flames from spreading across the table.

Patrick Adams starts forward, clearly shocked, but someone pulls him back with a stern warning. The judge makes a final note.

And the screen vanishes.

"Patrick Adams . . . Robot competition . . . His invention exploded. Unlucky."

Every limb is aching for some reason. I know it's only been a few minutes, but it's almost like the physical motions are fueling my mental travel. Like I'm biking my way to these moments and these memories that aren't captured anywhere else but in the minds of the boys I'm scrying on.

"Last one."

I pick up my speed again, leg muscles protesting. I have to lean forward and swivel my hips a little to keep the momentum. Patrick Bell's video appears on my phone. I watch him hit the full-court shot, again and again, until the scrying vision appears the same way it did with the others.

Patrick's walking through the hallways after school. Earlier today. *Everyone* is looking at him. I have a skin-prickling sensation. Goose bumps down the back of my neck, as if all those eyes are watching me, too. Patrick is clearly soaking in the stardom of hitting two game-winning shots in a row. I'm starting to follow him down the hallway, hoping to learn more, when he whips around. Maybe someone called his name? He looks almost directly at me. There's a slight frown on his face. Our eyes meet . . .

And then I feel something *shove* me away.

I hear Avery shout from somewhere nearby. It's the only warning I have before my back hits the hardwood floor. Thankfully, there's a stray pillow where my head would have landed. I roll onto one side, groaning as pain flashes across my entire lower back.

"Whoa, whoa, whoa!" Avery is saying. "What was that? Are you okay?"

My chest is heaving. Other aches and pains are blossoming out from the first one. I'm trying to stagger back to my feet when Avery drops to a knee beside me.

"Hey! Wait. How many fingers am I holding up?"

"Zero. You always hold up zero."

Avery laughs. "True. But are you sure you're okay?"

I take my feet. That was *weird*. The way that Patrick Bell turned to look at me. The way that I was *shoved* out of the vision—so hard that it knocked me down in real life? I'm still groaning away the pain as I reach for the guide book. I'm scanning the page about scrying, looking for an explanation, when I smell something in the air. The unexpected scent of fresh cookies.

"Did we put food in the oven?"

Avery frowns. "What? No . . ."

I sniff the air. It's still hanging there. A tantalizing scent.

"You don't smell that?"

"Okay. Now you're worrying me. Should I call your mom?"

"No . . . Hold on . . ."

I flip to the next page, finger tracing the words, and the answer is waiting there. It's not written in bold or anything, but it practically jumps off the page and waves a hand in my face.

Keep in mind, scrying is similar to looking through a telescope. There is only one access point for the accessible vision. If someone already has their eye to the lens—

attempting to push one's way forward and take a look might be met with aggression by the other seer in question. As silly as it sounds, there is a pretty firm "finders keepers" policy. The seer who arrived first will have the strongest hold on the lens, and thus on the subject.

The words come blurting out before I can stop them.

"There's another seer!"

CHAPTER TEN

Family Tree

After Avery leaves, the first thing I do is look through our family tree in the Cleary Family Guide Book.

It's kind of weird to see the black *X*s that announce the deceased. Grammy—always thinking ahead—marked an *X* on her own name before saving me last year. It has my eyes sweeping painfully away, on to the unmarked names. The "unmagical" generations are listed. Grammy had four children. My mom is the oldest of the bunch. Her sister Corabel came second, and had children the earliest: Mary and Martha. I make a note to call both of them.

Next is Genevieve. She had three children, but only one girl—and thus only one seer. I've only ever seen them at family reunions. Maybe once a year, but as I scan the listed dates of birth, I don't have to do much math to figure out that my cousin—Addie—is still way too young to have had her first vision. "It couldn't be her . . . so . . . who else . . ."

The fourth sibling is Gerald. Mom's estranged brother. I've never met him or any of his kids. Apparently, there's a very long story about a set of old golf clubs. The kind of small argument that turned into a much bigger argument. Grammy still dutifully listed off his children—but James, Geoff, and John are all boys.

"No magic for them . . ."

Next, I scan through Grammy's extended family. Her siblings had kids, and their kids had kids. My final tally comes out to just six others. Counting myself, Martha, Mary, and Addie, that makes ten. Ten children in our generation who will possess the powers that the Cleary family has passed down through the centuries. But as far as I can tell, none of the others even live in the same state as me. First I start with the cousins I've actually met.

The phone rings a few times, then an absurdly loud voice. "Celia! What's up?!"

There's a ton of chatter in the background, like she's in the middle of a massive crowd.

"Hey, Martha! Not much. Quick question."

"Shoot."

"I got pushed out of a vision just now," I say, trying to ignore the random chants in the background. Maybe she's at a football game? "By *another* seer. What's your scent again?"

She makes a thoughtful noise. "Old-lady store, remember? And Mary is waffle cones."

"Oh. Right. Thanks! Okay, I'll talk to you soon."

I hang up before Martha can ask what this is all about. Mary's number is listed right beneath hers in my phone. I tap it. I thought the smell earlier was freshly baked cookies, but waffle cones are close enough that I've got to at least ask her. It rings a few times before a tired voice answers.

"Yeah?"

"Sorry, Mary. It's Celia. Were you sleeping?"

"Not on purpose. What's up?"

"So I was working on that same vision, the doomsday one, when I got *shoved* out of the glimpse. You haven't had a vision lately, have you? Of an eighth-grade boy? A basketball player?"

I can hear her moving around. Likely sitting up in bed. Something falls and she mutters a curse. I'm thinking that maybe I've stumbled upon the connection, but Mary answers.

"No, nothing like that. You got shoved out of the actual vision? How?"

"I don't know! It was like . . . I got pushed. A big mental push."

I can almost hear Mary's mind spinning. "Hmm. Usually the first seer maintains control when two people are trying to look at the same future. I know there's also something about magic amplifying with multiple involved seers. There can be some weird side effects. The important thing is that someone else already has eyes on what's happening. . . . You know, there are a few second and third cousins we've lost track of over the years. Did you look up the family tree? It's on page—"

"One twenty-three. I know. I've written all the possible names down from our family."

"If the other seer is from our family."

The words that were on the tip of my tongue stutter to a halt. I hadn't even considered that possibility. Grammy always hinted at other magics, but the Cleary Family Guide Book is hyperfocused on *our* family's experience of magic. I can't remember reading too many discussions about what powers other seers have—or even direct mentions of what other families might exist.

"Do you really think there's someone else out there?"

"Sure," Mary says. "Grammy always said that most families let their magic fade away, but that doesn't mean it's all completely gone. But let's stay focused on what we can control. Check off the list of our family members first. If it's not a distant cousin, then we can worry about other families. . . . Hey. Do you want me to come down next weekend? I can help you research?"

I shake my head. "Mary, you've got . . . I don't know . . . college stuff."

She laughs. "Please. You're a two-hour trip! And I have more time in college than I ever did in high school. I'll clear my schedule, as long as you don't mind me sleeping there."

More of Grammy's advice is kicking in. Last year—and really my whole life—I'd have preferred to just try solving it on my own. One of Grammy's notes in the guide book was that I'm stronger with people beside me. And Mary's super smart. Besides, she actually knows what it's like to be a seer.

"If it's not a big deal, I'd love for you to visit."

"Perfect. Why don't you try to call the other relatives?" Mary asks, forming an action plan. "I'm going to figure out if there's any way for us to determine *when* the point of no return is for your doomsday. That seems pretty important. Especially if someone else is limiting your access to normal visions. Once we know that, we'll know how quickly we need to take action. Unless you feel like it's about to happen? What does your intuition tell you?"

The guide book talks about that idea all the time. For a

seer, intuition is everything. Our visions aren't just black and white. There's a ton of gray, and our *feelings* help us navigate that gray.

"I don't feel like it's going to happen tomorrow," I answer. "But I do feel like it's starting. *Something* is about to happen, and I'd like to know a lot more about what's going on before it does."

"Got it," Mary says. "Okay. Tell your mom I'm coming. And hey, Celia?"

I take a deep breath. "Yeah?"

"You know I'm always a phone call away, right?"

I nod, then remember she can't see me. "Yeah."

"All right. Love you, cousin. See you this weekend."

And just like that, I've got reinforcements coming. It gives me a little boost of confidence. I head downstairs, knowing Mom will be home in less than an hour. That's plenty of time to call a few people. I find the family contact book down in the drawer where Grammy always kept it. Her familiar scrawl dances across every page. Mom stopped adding to it years ago, using the data in her phone instead, but most of the numbers I'll need are in here. I pull up the guide book, double-check the list of who is alive, and dial the first number.

"Uhh . . . yes . . . hello. I'm hoping to speak with a . . . Cornelia Lockett?"

CHAPTER ELEVEN

Reconnaissance

In just one night, I check off every possible name in our family but two.

The first potential suspect is Grammy's youngest sister—Uva. Based on the date of birth listed for her, it's likely that she's still alive. The second possibility is Uva's unnamed grandchild. The note in that section of the family tree simply says: *Born in Oklahoma? Winter 2010?* That would make her just a little younger than me. But there's no name to look up. There's not even a confirmation of whether it was a boy or a girl. When I called the number listed in Grammy's notebook for Uva, it was disconnected. I file it away as one loose thread for Mary and me to tug on later.

The bigger question: Does the other seer know Patrick is on the verge of a doomsday scenario? If they're more experienced than me—like Uva—they're probably already on the case, figuring out how to fix everything. But what if it's a seer who's younger than me? What if this is their very first vision? Just like my first one was of Jeffrey dying. If they don't have someone like Grammy to help them, things could go downhill really fast.

Ideally I would spend all the next day investigating, but there's this thing called *school* that I still have to attend. I get up that morning with one silver lining: being at school guarantees that all three of the Patricks will be somewhere nearby. On the bus, Jeffrey plunks down next to me and notices I'm in the middle of doing a worksheet.

"Need some help?"

I shake my head. "No, I just didn't have time to do it last night."

As the bus bumps along, I start shading the next section of

my map. Jeffrey is surprisingly quiet. Usually he wants to tell me about his practice from the night before, or share some hilarious video he discovered. The ongoing silence allows me to focus, though, and by the time the bus pulls into school, I've completed twelve of the thirteen assigned questions.

"Hey," I say, looking over at Jeffrey. "How was practice last night?"

He shrugs. "It was practice."

I frown a little at the response. He's looking around the bus, craning his neck as we pull into the bus drop-off. It's like he can't wait to leave or something. This is so weird.

"Is everything okay?" I ask.

Jeffrey shrugs again, and I barely resist reaching out and smacking his shoulder. I've never seen him act like this before. Was it something I said?

"I'm fine," he answers.

"You've been so quiet."

"Yeah? Well, I didn't want to distract you."

"I know. I had to do my homework, but we still could have talked. All I'm doing is coloring a map . . ."

"Right. Well. You got this one wrong." He taps my paper. "And don't tell me this one appeared because of some magic spell. I literally had to sit here and *watch* you write it."

I'm so shocked by his words that I almost don't notice what I got wrong. My eyes scan the map before landing on the spot on the page he tapped. I mislabeled the *Outer Banks*. Instead, I wrote the *Patrick Bell Banks*. It's so embarrassing that I look back up, ready to explain, only to realize Jeffrey is already at the front of the bus. He slid past other students before the doors opened, and now there's an entire crowd of people between us.

It's a total misunderstanding. He knows I've been doing research on Patrick. My mind *was* distracted, but as I follow everyone else off the bus, searching for Jeffrey, I realize he must think this is more than a normal distraction. More than just magic. This time the name Patrick is written in *my* handwriting on the worksheet. Jeffrey must think I have a crush on him.

There's a small part of me that understands. Every time Jeffrey smiles at another girl, I get a little nervous. But another part of me wishes he would have just asked me. It would have been easy to explain what's really going on. By the time the crowd clears at the bottom of the bus stairs, he's already gone. I follow the other students inside, half hoping Jeffrey's still waiting at the usual spot where we always part ways in the morning.

But he's not there. I can feel tears welling up a little. I force myself to take a deep breath. It's just a mistake. I'll explain it all later. It will be fine. I keep searching for him, just in case, but there's no sign that he stuck around. Instead, my eyes land on Patrick Bell.

He's standing at the center of the nearest locker bay. And he's *glowing*. Not just happy, but literally *glowing* with golden light. It is the weirdest thing I've ever seen in my life. A circle of students surrounds him. It's clear he's the center of attention. And no wonder—he looks like a second sun. Other students are stopping, rubbernecking, until the crowd has doubled in size. I'm finally close enough to hear what he's saying.

"Yeah. Just fifty pairs released in the whole world!" I realize he's pointing down to his shoes. That's what everyone is crowded around to look at? They're not staring at the weird glow? "And the lottery had over five hundred thousand people enter. It was wild. I couldn't believe the email when I saw it. These shoes are *amazing*."

I glance down. He's wearing some kind of retro high-tops with gold-and-fuchsia slashes running along the sides. They look pretty cool, I guess, but not cool enough to explain why everyone is congratulating him left and right. I hear the kid next to me mutter under his breath.

"Those are the coolest shoes I've ever seen," he says.

I frown. "Really?"

He doesn't hear my question, though. He's practically hypnotized by Patrick, leaning forward to try to hear what the school's most interesting boy will say next. So is the rest of the crowd. Everyone looks entranced by him. Until the minute bell rings its warning overhead. That sharp, repeating sound breaks the . . .

"Spell," I realize. "This is *magic*."

The golden light surrounding him makes so much more sense. No wonder no one else reacted to it. I'm the only one who can see it. Usually I can only see my own magic. So why...

The scrying spell.

This must be an aftereffect. I'm still seeing traces of other magic. And there is no denying that Patrick Bell is smothered in the glow of a spell. I stand there for a second, knowing I need to get to first period, before deciding to follow Patrick Bell instead. I don't have any classes with him, so I'm pretty sure his classroom won't be close to mine. I ignore the fact that I might be late, trailing him down the hall instead. There are four other kids walking with him, all a step behind, like he's the president or something. Every time he makes a joke, they laugh. Every time he says he doesn't like something, they nod. Of course, they don't like it either.

Could he really be the other seer?

I've never read anything about a boy in our family having the gift. But I also never asked Grammy about other branches of magic. What if there are *other* families out there? Families where the magic manifests in some other way? I follow him and notice that even the teachers waiting outside their classroom doors take note when Patrick passes them. They offer nods and smiles. One actually waves at him, and Patrick waves back.

Whatever spell he's using, it's a really strong one.

I keep following Patrick and his group of friends. All the way to the end of the hallway. Some of the teachers are checking the watches on their wrists, waiting for the tardy bell to officially ring so they can close their doors. But the sound doesn't come.

It doesn't ring until the exact moment Patrick Bell steps inside his classroom. It's a little eerie. The way his feet cross the threshold of the doorway, and *then* the bell rings right on cue. His teacher waves him to his seat, grinning at his good luck. All I can do is stand in the hallway as my stomach does backflips. I'm still staring when a flicker of movement catches my eye from deeper inside the classroom. It's Jeffrey. His face is bright red. He's watching me watch Patrick. I offer the most awkward wave in existence before whipping back in the other direction.

I can feel sweat forming on my forehead. I have no idea how I'm going to explain to Jeffrey what happened, but right now, it feels like the smaller of two problems. If the vision I had is supposed to be connected to a doomsday scenario, then why does it seem like Patrick Bell is the *luckiest* person in our school? The game-winning shots, the shoe lottery, the tardy bell practically waiting for him. It seems like the entire world is bending in Patrick's direction. Why is that such a bad thing?

A throat clears. One of the assistant principals is standing in front of me.

"Late for class, Miss Cleary?"

Guess I'm not as lucky.

A surprisingly normal school day follows.

There are no ill omens in the air. No flashes of a new vision. No sightings of any of the Patricks. It's like I've gone back in time a few days to when I didn't know there was any doomsday prophecy happening at all. I just wish I could reset what happened with Jeffrey, too. The quiet day has me more on edge. I can't get the strange thought out of my head: *Patrick Bell is some kind of seer.*

I keep thinking back to my scrying vision of him. I was

following Patrick Bell down the hall when he turned around. It was like he was looking right at me. And *then* I got pushed out of the vision. I didn't think about the possibility that it could have been him pushing me out. I'm also not sure how to prove any of this. It's not like I can just go up and ask: *Hey, do you also do magic?*

School ends, and I find myself face-to-face with the decision I've debated all day. I can head to the buses, explain what happened to Jeffrey, and make sure he still likes me.

Or I can follow my gut feeling that something big is about to happen. Something connected to my vision. The debate has me chewing on my lower lip. After a few seconds, I turn away from the buses and start walking toward the gymnasium. I text Jeffrey and tell him not to wait for me. I find myself hoping that I'm not making a huge mistake.

The basketball team has practice after school. I know I can't do anything if I don't learn more about Patrick Bell. But when I reach the gym, it's empty. I frown at the abandoned court—a stray rack of basketballs in one corner—until spotting Harper Ross. He's literally the tallest kid at our school, so it's kind of hard *not* to spot him. He's got his basketball hoodie on and his bag slung around his neck.

"Yo!" Harper calls. "Wait up!"

I watch as he jogs to catch up with someone down the hallway. Half of the basketball team is headed that way. Even at a distance, I spot that little glow of golden light around Patrick. I follow them down the hall, worried they're about to leave for an away game. That would mean I have no chance to spy on Patrick and learn more about him. Not if they load up the bus and drive somewhere else in the county.

But thankfully, they don't head for the back bus lot. Instead, they take the school's side entrance, through the double doors and outside. I follow them like a spy in a movie.

It's bright and a little warm. I watch as the basketball team heads for the marked crosswalk. It's a busy road, but when they press the button, lights flash and everyone driving by knows to stop and let students cross. The boys wait a few seconds before walking. I spot Patrick Bell, still with a slight glow, at the front of the group.

There's a small parking lot waiting for them on the

other side. I have to hustle to keep up with them. I'm about thirty yards behind them. Clearly, this is a normal routine. Something they've all done before. Maybe they always have a little time between the end of school and practice? There's a row of buildings linked in a semicircle. I count four different stores, and it takes a second to figure out which one the basketball players are visiting.

Not the laundromat. Not the fine-dining Italian restaurant. Not the yoga workshop.

No, they aim for the entrance of a little shop on the corner. I glance up at the sign and go completely still: *Spellbound Bakery*. A bell chimes as they go inside. Before I can follow them, a scent wafts out to me. Strong, even in the slight wind. Familiar, too, because I smelled it last night before being shoved out of the vision: *freshly baked cookies.* It's the same scent I encountered when the journal first opened too. Even though it could get awkward in such a small space, I don't really feel like I have any other option.

I follow them inside.

CHAPTER TWELVE

Spellbound Bakery

I'm not sure what I was expecting.

A cauldron? The name of the bakery had me thinking that there'd be an obvious-looking witch waiting inside, tapping black-painted fingernails on the counter as she took orders. I smile a little, remembering people's expectations when they came to see Grammy for a reading.

Instead of a proper seer, though, there's an average-looking person named Dave at the cash register. He eyes the crowd of basketball players with slight annoyance. I stand behind them, hidden from view, and quietly take in the rest of the store.

There's not much to take in. The floor is faded hardwood. Tables are scattered around. One long table that's meant to be shared by customers, and then smaller circular tables ringing the edges of the room. The front window looks out over the cracked-asphalt parking lot. The name of the bakery has been painted large on one of the exposed interior walls. I note that the only indication of "magic" in their logo is the *o* in *Spellbound*. It's colored in to look like a crescent moon. It feels like a pretty big coincidence that Patrick would lead me to a place like this.

Coincidence? Grammy's voice scolds. *Might as well be a bull's-eye.*

A shiver runs down my spine. It's the first time in a while that I've actually heard her voice in my memories. I know her advice is waiting for me in the guide book. Sometimes I think about the things she used to say to me. But this is the first time since she passed away that I actually could hear her again— the way I used to when she could sit down and talk with me.

Her words have my attention swinging back to the main target of my investigation. Patrick Bell is at the front of the line, but he waves his buddies ahead of him. They go up one at a time, buying the cheapest things on the menu. Dave rings them up one by one, clearly not thrilled by the pack of players hooting and hollering in front of him. There's only one other customer, seated by the front window.

Patrick keeps waiting. I'm getting awkwardly close to him, close enough to smell that overpowering scent of cookies in the air. And then the double doors behind the counter open. A girl our age comes out of the back. She has dark, curly hair on the verge of ringlets, all tied up with a floral headband. Her skin is light brown, though I imagine in the summer she has an even darker complexion. She's really cute, but I can tell just from her posture that she's painfully shy. The way she hunches in on herself. The way her eyes dart to and from the group of basketball players. It's even in the blush that colors her cheeks as she slides a tray of cookies into the glass display case.

Patrick waves. She blushes even more, signaling for him

to wait. I watch her duck into the back room again. A second later, she comes out with an absolutely delicious-looking chocolate chip cookie. I pretend like I'm eyeing the menu, but I'm totally eavesdropping.

"Seriously, these are the *best*," Patrick says. "You sure it's cool? I don't have to pay?"

The girl nods, like nothing in the world would please her more than to sneak this free cookie to Patrick Bell. She mumbles, "I made it just for you . . ."

Seriously? I think. *Is this his magic? Everyone just gives him whatever he wants?*

"I shouldn't eat these before practice, but they're my good luck charm. Thanks again."

He offers a bright smile. I'm watching both of them, trying to get some hint of how he's actually using his magic, when I realize that someone else in the room is trying to get my attention. It's Dave from behind the counter. The rest of the line has already ordered. I'm the only one left.

"Can I help you?"

I step forward, but it's only when I look up at the menu

that I remember I didn't bring my wallet to school today. "Oh . . . whoops . . . just one second . . ."

I fumble through my book bag, scrambling to find any leftover change. I manage to scrounge up sixty-five cents, which is enough to buy exactly *zero* of the items on the menu. Dave looks at me like I'm an even worse customer than the basketball team, and that's when Patrick Bell sweeps forward.

"Here. I can spot you a dollar."

"Umm . . ."

It's so awkward to come face-to-face with the boy I'm here to spy on. The boy who is likely at the center of a doomsday prophecy. It's also really bright. Almost blinding. Like all the golden light surrounding him is focused on me, whispering to me. But knowing about the spell makes it easier for me to resist the effect. That's something Grammy taught me.

"Thanks."

Before I can turn around and pick something, I catch a glimpse of the other girl over Patrick's right shoulder. She was all nervous smiles a second ago, but now she looks *furious*. I frown before realizing that Patrick Bell has chosen to stay with me, rather than walk back to his conversation with her. I've unintentionally stolen him away.

"You go to our school, right?"

I nod. "Yeah. Celia. I'm in eighth grade."

"Cool," he says. "I'm Patrick. I play basketball . . ."

He taps the emblem on his chest, like it wasn't completely obvious. I nod before remembering that Dave is still waiting on my order. "Thanks. For the dollar. I'll pay you back."

Even with his money, I still have to stick to the cheaper items on the menu. I order a basic sugar cookie, pass over the cash, and head straight for the nearest table. I feel hot under my sweater, knowing that both Patrick and the girl are probably staring at me. I try to play it cool. All the basketball players are lounging at the main table, laughing about nothing. The customer near the front window is already fishing through his book bag, untangling his headphones. I sit there for a minute, as patient as I can be, until it feels like enough time has passed to risk a glance.

Patrick Bell has taken his free cookie and joined the basketball crew. Dave looks bored behind the counter. But just beyond him, prowling back and forth like some kind of annoyed bird, is the other girl. Her eyes aren't on Patrick. They're on me. She's upset because I interrupted her moment with him. I do my best to ignore her glare. It's not easy. The place is tiny.

I'm pretending my sugar cookie is the most fascinating thing in the entire world when it happens. The magic around Patrick *flashes* even brighter. No one else can see it, but I can. The light is so bright that he looks briefly like an angel in my second sight. A single thread of that same golden light weaves overhead, lashing across the room. Patrick is eating his cookie and seems completely unaware of what's happening. It's weird, though, because it looks like . . .

"The magic is flowing the other way."

I cover my mouth, but thankfully, no one heard. No one else is seeing magic stretching overhead. Not even Patrick Bell because he *isn't* the source. The magic isn't flowing out from him. It's flowing *toward* him. Which means it's coming from . . .

My eyes lock on the other girl. She's heading back to the

kitchen, but there is no doubt in my mind that the sudden burst of magic came from her. *You're the source! You're the seer!* I rush over to the front counter and try to keep my voice low.

"Hi! Can I speak to the baker?"

Dave raises an eyebrow. "Why do you want to see the baker?"

"I wanted to give them my compliments. On the cookie."

I'm pretty sure that's a thing? I feel like Mom did that once. It was at a fancy restaurant, and technically she spoke with the chef, but maybe it's a rule that also can be applied at random neighborhood bakeries? Dave looks like he's never heard anything more absurd. He glances at the sugar cookie in my hand before sighing.

"Skyler! A customer wants to talk to you!"

Skyler. Her name is Skyler. Maybe she's the unnamed cousin?

There's a bang from the kitchen. She shoves eagerly back through the double doors because I think she's hoping Patrick has returned to talk to her. When she sees that it's me, her jaw tightens. Dave switches places with her, heading back into the kitchen to get something that's beeping. She looks at me like I'm the last person in the world she wants to talk to.

"Well? What is it?"

"Your name is Skyler?"

She nods. "Skyler Dawkins. Did you need something?"

"I need to know . . ."

It always feels weird to say it out loud, but I'm so excited by the possibility of having someone else nearby who knows what it's like to be me. I lower my voice to a whisper.

"I need to know how long you've been able to do magic."

CHAPTER THIRTEEN

Good Luck Charm

Skyler sputters. "I—wait, what?"

Grammy used to say that you could always tell a lot about someone in the moment *before* they've fully processed something. Before they can pretend or put their guard up or any of that. And one thing is very clear: Skyler does not know *anything* about her magic. I'm certain that she's doing *something*. The magical thread I saw in the air was clearly coming from her, and clearly connected to Patrick. Could she really be performing magic without knowing it?

"How do you know him? Patrick Bell?"

It's the worst follow-up question I could ask. Skyler blushes violently. She swipes a stray hair behind one ear, darts a look over to the table of basketball players, then shrugs like it's not a big deal.

"We go to school together."

For some reason, that surprises me. I'm not sure why I thought she went somewhere else, though. She's working in a bakery that's literally across the street from our school. It makes sense.

"Right. Sorry. I know this is confusing, but . . . have you . . . seen anything? Like dreams? Or visions? Maybe, I don't know, glimpses of . . . umm . . . the future?"

As soon as the words leave my mouth, I feel like the *weirdest* person in the world. I've always loved Grammy, always loved this part of who I am. The wild magic that courses through my veins is so cool. But nothing sounds stranger than asking if someone has *seen the future.* Skyler's looking at me like I'm about to walk her through all of my theories on alien abduction.

"Sorry. I'm doing a really bad job of explaining what I'm talking about. . . ."

There's a little *chime*. I glance back and see an older couple walking into the store. Skyler smooths her apron and looks ready to move back behind the counter. I know I don't have much time. I'm trying to figure out what to say when I remember the journal. All of those *Patrick*s scrawled over the page. I quickly wrestle with my book bag, shoving folders aside, and pull the notebook out. Before Skyler can get rid of me, I open it up to the right page. She freezes in place.

"We need to talk. About *this*."

Twenty different emotions flicker across her face. Anger and confusion and embarrassment and more. But when I shove the notebook back into my book bag and head for a corner table, she throws on a plastered smile and welcomes the two customers behind me. They're interested in ordering some kind of cake. All the basketball players have finished their snacks and are getting ready to head back to school for practice. I briefly consider following them—following Patrick Bell. But every instinct in the world tells me that the real answer to the mystery I've been unraveling is right here inside this bakery.

Skyler Dawkins is the center of the doomsday prophecy.

I text my mom that I'm finishing up homework at the bakery. She offers to pick me up on her way home from work in an hour. I go through most of my language arts project before realizing the rest of the bakery is pretty much empty. All the customers are gone. Dave's got a clipboard behind the counter and looks like he's counting inventory. It takes seeing him from this angle to realize that he and Skyler are related. They have the same nose, the same chin. That must be how she got this job in the first place. Most kids our age aren't allowed to work, unless it's for a family business. That's clearly the case here.

I wait until Skyler appears again. She sees me looking her way and says something to Dave. She cleverly covers her approach by picking up a tray of samples.

"Hello. Do you want to try our new lemon-twist meringues?"

She stands there, chin slightly raised, clearly annoyed. I

accept one of the treats. It's delicious. Skyler looks like she's considering going straight back to the kitchen. Instead, she lowers her voice to a hissed whisper. "Where did you get that journal?"

I reach for the notebook and open it to the page in question.

"I know this will be hard to believe, but I'm a seer. My whole family . . . we're magical. These appeared in my journal the other day. Something important is about to happen to Patrick. He might be in danger. I've been trying to track down the source. Do you recognize the handwriting?"

Her jaw tightens. "Yeah. It's . . . it's mine. But this doesn't make any sense. I wrote all of these in different journals. On bathroom walls . . ." She traces the notebook with a finger. "How could they *all* be written in the same place? And why would they be in *your* journal?"

It's an accusation. I can tell she's still trying to figure out how to feel about this. I know there's a lot of talk at our school about who has a crush on who. I'm pretty sure that Patrick Bell has figured out that Skyler likes him by now. After all, he's the only basketball player she offered a free cookie. But offering a cookie is not the same thing as confessing that you've been writing someone's name in your journal over and over. That feels way more personal.

"Look, I like Patrick," Skyler bravely admits. "He's been coming in here ever since the basketball season started. He used to come by himself. I thought he was sweet. He told me he didn't really know any of the other basketball players. He hadn't made friends yet. So he always came here to kill time before practice. He was really cute. After a while, he started bringing half the team with him. . . ."

She glances back at Dave, but he's busy stocking shelves.

"I thought he liked me too. I hope he still . . . I don't know. Everything changed."

I lean forward. *Everything changed* are two words that have my seer instincts on alert. "How?"

She shrugs. "He got super popular. I was kind of hoping he'd ask me to the winter dance that's coming up. But I feel like a lot of girls have crushes on him now. . . ."

Skyler gives me a quick look, like I might be in that category. I hold up my hands innocently.

"I'm already dating someone."

She looks relieved. I'm still trying to mentally piece everything together. Skyler's words line up with what I've researched. Patrick Bell? Clearly popular. I think about the crowd around him at school. The way everyone praised his new shoes. It also lines up with the fact that he wasn't a starter on the basketball team. Not at first. But what does the golden glow have to do with all of that?

"Is there anything else?" I ask. "Any weird dreams? Coincidences? Déjà vu?"

Skyler looks pretty skeptical. I'm sure this is the strangest conversation that she's ever had. "Not really . . . well . . . there's one thing . . ."

"What?"

She shakes her head. "It's not like . . . I didn't *see* anything. No offense. I've never met someone who thinks they can . . . see visions or whatever."

"What happened?" I repeat, because if she didn't grow up thinking about the magic and knowing it existed, it's possible she would believe her abilities were just good instincts or something.

"Well, one day Patrick came in after school. He was having a really bad day. I guess he messed up in his basketball game the night before. I wanted to cheer him up. So I went back into the kitchen and made my favorite recipe. Uncle Dave doesn't sell them. They use too many of the fancy ingredients, but they're *really* good cookies.

"I made one for Patrick." She hesitates now, and it's clear this is something she's been thinking about for a while. "It was right before practice. He said he'd probably be sick if he ate a cookie. But I promised him it would be his good luck charm. I really wanted to make him feel better. It worked. He had a great practice. So I made him one the next day . . . and the next day . . ."

A single phrase sets off alarm bells in my head. *Good luck charm.* Charms are an entire branch of magic for some seers. In fact, the concept is so popular that it's dripped into the lives and thoughts of normal people too. Good luck and bad luck. Normal people don't realize there are literal charms that can be cast to change someone's luck. Especially if a seer has a knack for it. I know there are tons of recipes related to luck in the Cleary Family Guide Book.

It has me thinking back to the flash of magic I saw between the two of them. The way that the thread appeared in the air right as Patrick ate the cookie that Skyler made for him.

"I know," Skyler is saying. "It sounds ridiculous. But he's been so *lucky* ever since I started making him cookies. I don't know. It's like everything in his life is going right . . . which also means that he's not as interested in me. Kind of like he doesn't need me, now that everyone else likes him."

Everything in his life is going right.

Becoming a starter on the basketball team. Hitting game-winning shots. Winning a pair of shoes in a special lottery. Even the bell waited for him to get to class before it rang. It's all clicking into place. I'm about to tell Skyler my theory when the front door chimes. Mom leans inside just far enough to spot me sitting there. She waves her phone. I look down and see I've missed a bunch of texts from her. She was probably waiting outside in the car—and I can tell from the way she's standing there that she's not planning on waiting any longer. I pack up my stuff, even though I'd prefer to pick Skyler's brain for the rest of the afternoon. There's one big question I do need to ask.

"How many of those cookies have you made for Patrick?" I ask. "Your favorite ones."

Skyler shrugs. "I don't know. Like twenty of them?"

That explains the golden light I saw surrounding him. If Skyler's been giving him good luck charms, the magic might have built up over time. Each cookie would add on to the spell. But that just leads me to another big question. One that I can't ask Skyler because I doubt she would understand any of this. If Patrick Bell is so lucky—if everything is going his way—then why is the doomsday prophecy centering on him? It seems like he's experiencing the *opposite* of a disaster.

I need to get home and look in the guide book for answers.

As I finish packing, I reach for my journal. Very

deliberately, I rip out the page with all the scribbled *Patrick*s. "I'll let you have this, if you promise to do one thing."

Skyler's hand was already reaching out. I'm sure she was eager to secure a piece of evidence that could be very, very embarrassing for her. "What is it?"

"Don't make Patrick any more of those cookies."

She nods once. I scribble in the top corner before folding the page and handing it to her.

"If you think of anything else, my phone number is in that top corner."

When she takes the paper, I head for the door.

Skyler calls after me. "Wait. Aren't you going to tell me what's going on?"

"Tomorrow. We can talk tomorrow. Just don't give him any more cookies."

And with that weird demand, I head out the front door of the Spellbound Bakery.

CHAPTER FOURTEEN

Less Lucky

As Mom pulls out of the parking lot, my mind is racing.

"... was that a new friend of yours?"

"Huh?"

"The girl in the coffee shop? It looked like you were exchanging numbers."

"Oh. Um. Kind of. We just met."

"That's nice! I love your friend group, but it's always nice to meet new people."

Not just a new person, I think excitedly. *A new seer. Someone who's like me.*

I keep that part to myself, though. Mom's always felt like magic was foreign territory for her, an unknowable place. Learning there's another seer at my school would be a lot to take on. Besides, I need to figure out what's happening before I jump to any more conclusions.

". . . Corabel and I talked on the phone earlier. She was glad that Mary was coming to visit. Said this semester's been tough on her. She's such a sweet girl."

I nod. "Yeah, I'm excited she's coming. . . ."

Mom turns at the next stop sign. It's hard to focus on our conversation. I keep seeing that golden magic wrapped around Patrick Bell like a shield. If it really was the result of a good luck charm, Skyler's been providing him a *lot* of extra luck. I need to figure out exactly what kind of magic she's using. I also need to figure out how that magic could go wrong. As always, I'm hoping the guide book—and Grammy's notes—will have the answers.

I hear Mom make a *hmm* sound. Her dark brows furrow together. There are brake lights ahead. "Must be an accident," she says. "There's never traffic here."

We slow to a standstill. "Mm-hmm."

"Distracted, honey?"

"Huh?"

She grins at me. "What's on your mind?"

"I'm trying to solve something. . . . There's this vision. It's like a big puzzle. I've figured out most of the pieces, and now I just have to figure out the rest. I wish Grammy was here."

I didn't even realize I was thinking it, but the words come out like a ready-formed thought. Mom and I both avoid eye contact. We sit in silence as the car moves forward a few feet at a time. I can't help feeling slightly guilty. The one secret I've kept from Mom is about *how* Grammy died. She doesn't know about Jeffrey, or that Grammy eventually sacrificed herself to save me. For the second time, I consider telling her everything, but she speaks first.

"Me too. Sometimes . . . I feel like I'm having little conversations with her. Imagining what she would have to say about this or that." She laughs to herself. "You know, sometimes it feels like she told me things, when she was still here, because she *knew* what was going to happen. I had to fire someone at work this week. It was a really hard decision, but then I remembered something she said, a while ago, and it gave me so much comfort. Is that . . . could that be how it worked? Her gift? Would she have known about events that far in advance?"

I realize Mom is genuinely curious. Sometimes I forget that she doesn't know about our world. Doesn't really know how Grammy's gift—or mine—really works. I smile over at her.

"Actually, yeah. I wouldn't be surprised if Grammy did something like that. The same thing happens to me. I hear her voice all the time."

It hits me that I started really *hearing* her voice again when I met Skyler. It was like meeting another seer unlocked that side of my brain. Instead of just feeling the pain of Grammy's absence, it's like all of her wisdom came thundering back to life.

"She gave me little pieces of advice," I say. "Like she knew I'd need her help along the way."

We're quiet again for a while. A painful thought hits me.

"I hope I don't lose her voice. The sound of it."

Mom nods. "You won't. We'll help each other remember. Okay?"

I nod, but now I can't look directly at Mom. I'm too close to crying, and eye contact never helps when you're trying to hold back the floodgates. Besides, I feel like one glance is all it would take to confess everything that happened last year. I almost want to tell her that the reason Grammy's absence is so painful, besides the fact that she's not here, is that I still feel like I'm responsible for her death. As the quiet stretches, I wonder if maybe I'm *supposed* to tell Mom about what really happened. I know Grammy wouldn't want there to be a secret like this between us.

Our car has nosed forward enough that we finally reach the source of the traffic. The sight confirms there was an accident. Two cars in a fender bender. Not so bad that anyone is hurt, but there's debris scattered in one lane.

The front car is a massive truck. It looks like they got a few scratches on their back fender. The second car took most of the damage. It ran right into the back of the truck, and the entire hood popped up, bent at an odd angle. I'm squinting at the damage when I see the family to which the car belongs. A familiar figure stands at the center of the group.

"That's Patrick!"

Not Patrick Bell, though. I spot the long red hair and a skater's hoodie: Patrick Connors. He's standing safely in the median. A younger sibling is tucked in at his side. His mom stands there, shaking her head. A police officer is on the scene to interview everyone. Our car's progress takes us within twenty yards. Patrick Connors spots me craning my neck to look out the window. He looks away in embarrassment, and I finally realize it's probably not polite to stare. As I lean back in my seat, though, I catch a glimpse of the cast on his arm. It's a bright red color, and artwork has been scribbled all over it.

I remember that detail from the scrying vision. He broke his wrist while skateboarding. And now he's been in a car accident. I frown as we pass by them. Mom sighs. "That's so unlucky."

And the word rings in my head like a gong. It's like the echo of a familiar sound that twists right before it reaches your ears. Déjà vu but not. I know right away that it's another clue. Patrick Bell has been really lucky lately. And I'm pretty sure the reason he's been lucky is Skyler Dawkins. But what happens when someone starts getting extra luck? Is it possible that someone else gets less?

Not just one someone, I think. *Two people: Patrick Connors and Patrick Adams.*

"You know, you're a lot like her . . ."

Mom's words pull me out of my own thoughts.

"Who?"

"Grammy. That look you get when you're thinking. She always had the same expression. When her wheels were turning and she was on the verge of figuring something out. I always noticed it when she was reading that awful detective series. Remember those?"

"About the necromancers?"

We both laugh because those books were one of

Grammy's guiltiest pleasures. They always had steamy covers of guys with six-packs holding skulls. I can still picture her out on the back patio, eyebrows raised at whatever was happening in her book. When the laughter fades, my smile doesn't because Mom is right. I am on the verge of figuring something out.

Grammy would be proud.

CHAPTER FIFTEEN

Our Powers Combined

I'm buried under the covers in my room, flipping through the family guide book, when a knock sounds at the door. I'm expecting Mom to peek inside. The person who appears is already taller than Mom, athletic and muscular from off-season practice with her rowing team. Her blond ponytail bobs slightly as she crosses the room with two cups of tea in hand.

"Mary! You're here!"

She's wearing a school hoodie and leggings. I've always thought she was a natural beauty, even though college has clearly drained her a little. There are bags under her eyes and the slightest hesitation to her smile. Underneath all of that, however, is the same steady girl I've known since I was a little kid. The cousin who always held my hand and walked me around the pond at the old Cleary family farm.

"You must be exhausted," I say.

She sets my tea on the bedside table and shrugs. "The drive wasn't bad. And honestly, I haven't gone to sleep earlier than midnight all year. Besides, nothing can keep me from a good mystery. Come on. Catch me up on what's been happening. . . ."

So I do. It takes about thirty minutes to run through all the details. Mary is—first and foremost—a good student. She asks questions, takes notes in her own journal, and nods along through the entire story. She looked tired when she got here, but by the time I finish, it's like she's taken a few shots of espresso. Maybe that's partly due to the tea she's sipping? I'm pretty sure it has a lot more to do with the magic, though. She paces around the room. It's nice to have someone as excited about this as I am.

"Okay. I'm not even sure where to start," Mary says. "Because this is a *lot*. First, there's another seer. Another one of us! We talked about the fact that she could be from another family, but let's start with our family first. Any chance she's related?"

"Not sure. She'd have to be Uva's granddaughter. I didn't ask Skyler about that. Pretty sure I freaked her out enough with the whole magic journal thing. Didn't think that adding in a *We're actually related* reveal would be very fair."

"Good call." Mary nods. "Okay. Second: you've done *so* good, Celia. Scrying was a great idea. You're following your instincts and the clues and everything. You've got a knack for this. You're going to be such an amazing seer."

We've got the lights in the room dimmed, but I'm pretty sure she can still see the way that has me blushing. I've always looked up to Mary. Without Grammy at my side, I feel like I'm just winging it sometimes. Practicing something without really knowing if I'm any good. Her words are a reminder: I've made progress. I'm actually getting better at this.

"I'm not even bragging on you. It's just the truth," Mary

continues. "Based on all this, I'm pretty sure there are two big questions to ask. First, what kind of magic is Skyler doing? It *sounds* like a good luck charm, but we should probably triple-check just in case. And second . . ."

"How does a good luck charm go wrong?"

"Exactly. A doomsday is the *opposite* of lucky. So why is someone with extra doses of luck the center of a doomsday event? That's our biggest mystery."

Mary snatches the family guide and starts flipping through the pages. That's another admirable quality of hers. That lack of hesitation. Once she sets a course, she's full steam ahead. I guess that's why she makes such a good rower. She possesses an ability to push on toward a specific goal, no matter what. It's comforting to have someone like that at my side.

"I marked page thirty-three," I tell her. "There's a section that fits Skyler. It's all about Charmists. Apparently, they're seers who can *charm* events and people around them. Most of the time they offer just the slightest stroke of luck, but the best Charmists? They've changed the outcomes of the World Series, altered the fates of entire companies . . ."

Mary nods. "Got it . . . definitely fits . . . and good luck charms . . ."

"On the next page."

I already read that section but didn't see anything about potential negative consequences. Mary skims that section. "All right. This gives us a really good framework for her magic."

I sit up straighter. "It does?"

"This sentence near the end. *'The strongest charms combine the will of the seer with a normal object. Focus is required, as with all magic, but charms are actually fueled more by strong emotions than by ritual focus. That emotion must simply be channeled into a particular conduit. . . .'*" Mary looks up from the book. "You said she wanted to make Patrick feel better. She channeled that very strong desire—powered by her crush on him—into one delicious cookie. It's like he was literally eating good luck. And if Skyler's count is accurate, then he's been eating a *ton* of extra luck . . . Hold on. I'm pretty sure there's a section that lists out all the magical ratios. . . ."

I watch as she flips to the back of the book. There are a variety of tables and appendices there. Her fingers trace down the page until she stops dead. "Here. Look. A luck calculator."

"No way."

The entire page looks like a very old-school Excel worksheet. There are numbers running across each row with equations for determining luck, scrying distances, and even one that claims to calculate teleportation coordinates? I'm not bad at math—I'm actually pretty good at it—but what I'm looking at has my head spinning. There are a few equations that my brain can't even begin to break down.

Thankfully, Mary is here to offer her calculus-level computing skills. She arrives at a conclusion faster than I could multiply two numbers together.

"Well. That's not good." She traces her finger across the row. "Okay. The problem is the luck doesn't work in an additive way. It's not 2 + 2. It's a multiplier: 2 x 2 . . ."

I can't help pointing out the obvious. "Both of those equal 4."

Mary nods. "The first time, yes. But then you multiply 4 x 4. And then 16 x 16. And then 256 x 256. It goes on and on like that. Each time she charmed him with the cookie, it matched and multiplied the level of luck that already existed inside him. This is just a guess, but I'm pretty sure he's consumed about . . . 70 times the amount of good luck that a normal person should have. You said you could see it? In the air around him?"

"Yeah. It's hard to describe. It's almost like he was completely encircled by light."

Mary flips back to the charm section. "Let's see . . . here . . . 'Good luck magic—or positive karmic influence—should take on the slightest of golden sheens. To the eyes of an enhanced seer, it might appear like a vague glow or a fickle light that vanishes when you stare directly at it.' Does that sound right?"

I shake my head. "No. It was really bright. Almost blinding. And it didn't vanish. I could see it the whole time I followed him."

"That's a confirmation, then: he's walking around with

way too much. With that amount of luck, it's like he's permanently bending the universe to get what he wants in every situation."

It takes a second for me to remember the one detail that I left out.

"Wait! The other Patricks! There are two of them at our school."

Mary's half reading, half listening. "Oh?"

"And one of them was in a car accident tonight."

She looks up sharply. "Oh no . . . Is he . . ."

"He's fine. Sorry. Should have led with that. No one looked hurt, but when we passed by, Mom said it was unlucky. That word stuck in my head. Accidents *are* unlucky. And two days before that, he broke his arm skateboarding. I saw it happen. That was really unlucky too."

Mary's eyes light up. She connects the dots and starts frantically searching again. I'm kind of amazed that she knows the guide book so well—even though she lived a full state away from Grammy. Maybe she studied it one summer? She finds what she's looking for and turns the page to me. I read the title for this particular section, and feel my stomach start to turn.

Common Curses and Their Potential Cures

Beneath that is a note one of our former relative's added.

(Who labeled this chapter? There are like two cures in the whole section!!)

Mary points farther down the page. I groan out loud because *of course*, the thirteenth curse that's listed is *The Curse of Bad Luck*. It's one of the longer entries on the page. Mary and I both lean forward to read the curling script:

". . . there are clear and documented cases of actual Bad Luck curses. In these cases, circumstances should have led to a positive result, but fate unexpectedly causes something much worse to happen. The origins of such curses vary. Disturbing graves, repeating certain phrases in a mirror, or coordinating certain actions with lunar cycles—all of these can lead to Bad Luck.

Surprisingly, one of the most common causes has to do with the Law of Magical Balance. It is well known that

Bad Luck is the opposite of Good Luck. The first Charmists in our family didn't understand that charming one person might lead to the opposite effect for someone else. Help one person catch a winning touchdown, and you're also hurting the person who was supposed to stop them from scoring. Good Luck and Bad Luck go hand in hand.

We have also learned that Bad Luck spreads through proximity. It's transferred to someone with a clear link or closeness to the benefitting party. It's also worth noting that each person possesses a certain amount of natural luck. Once the entirety of their luck is drained, the curse would then echo to the next person. The most common target would be someone connected to both the recipient of the Good Luck and the individual who is now Luckless. . . .'"

"He's making them unlucky," I blurt. "Patrick Connors had the car accident and the broken arm. Maybe even the thing with the bathroom leaking! And Patrick Adams's robot exploded during a competition. So, this means the luckier Patrick Bell gets, the unluckier both of them are. . . ."

"And there's the explanation for your doomsday."

I frown. "What do you mean? I didn't see anything about a doomsday in there. . . ."

"Okay. Think about it this way. Patrick Bell is draining their luck. He's stealing it. That's obviously because of Skyler. She wrote that name down over and over again. The magic *linked* the three of them because they had the same name. He started stealing their luck. Eventually they're going to run out of luck completely."

My heart sinks. "And they'll . . . die?"

Mary looks a little shocked by that guess. Maybe she's forgotten that my first taste of magic was saving someone's life over and over again in a series of near-death accidents.

"I don't think it means they'll die. Well, they won't have any luck . . . so I guess bad things *will* happen to them. But they're more likely to be small things. Dog eats your homework. A tire goes flat. Missing the bus. Stuff like that. Look, there's a note right here. . . ."

She taps the spot on the page.

"Once he's drained them, the spell will expand. On and on, until he's drained as much Good Luck as one person can possibly possess. That chart we looked at listed an upper limit. I'd guess one person could steal the luck of about . . . two hundred other people. I'd have to run the full calculations, though."

"So . . . who would be next? After he drains the Patricks?"

Mary answers, "It says it right there in the text. Someone who knows the lucky *and* unlucky person. Think about it. Who would know all *three* Patricks?"

The realization hits. "Me?"

Mary reaches past me, though. She snags a book that I'd left on my bedside table. She turns it around so I can see the front cover. Our yearbook from last year.

"Not *just* you. How many people are in your eighth-grade class?" she asks.

The pieces all click together. I went over Mrs. Schubert's list the other day. We're not a huge school. "There *might* be two hundred people in our eighth grade . . . I'm not sure."

"Then the answer is all of them. If no one stops this spell . . . it will impact you and Jeffrey and all of your friends. Patrick Bell will take the luck from everyone. He'll be unstoppable."

"But how long would that last? A couple of weeks? The spell can't go on forever."

Mary shakes her head sadly.

"That's the problem. You said you saw the doomsday emblem. That marks a point of no return. Which means there's a point where he'll gain too much luck to be stopped. He will spend the rest of his life as the luckiest person in the world. Everything will go right for him . . . and while that's happening, the rest of you will be completely unlucky. Forever. But a point of no return also means that he can still be stopped. There's still hope."

I lean back against my bed's headboard, a little stunned. The movement rocks my bed just slightly. The bed nudges up against my nightstand. The tea that Mary set there—gone cold long before—crashes to the floor. White shards scatter from the spot. A puddle of tea starts spreading across the hardwood floor. One word comes to mind.

I don't say the word. Mary doesn't say the word. But we're both thinking it: *unlucky.*

CHAPTER SIXTEEN

A Meeting of Seers

For the first time in my life, I have a dream that's also a vision.

I can tell because that campfire scent fills the air. The entire scene around me is dark—and then suddenly it isn't. I'm seated at a table. I glance back over one shoulder and realize I'm in the Spellbound Bakery. The door has just chimed. Patrick Bell is frozen at the entrance. A playful smile is starting to stretch over his face. I can see the dimple forming on his right cheek. The light catches his hair, making the ordinary brown look like it's streaked with sunlight. Before

I can even stand up, though, and start examining the scene, I feel it again. Something *shoves* me back. Out of the vision.

And right out of my dream, too. I wake up with a start. Thankfully, the movement just sends me rolling on top of another pillow this time—instead of falling backward off my mom's Peloton. I take a few heaving breaths. This time, I know exactly who pushed me, even if she doesn't realize that she's doing it. My usual campfire scent is mingled with freshly baked cookies.

Skyler Dawkins is dreaming about Patrick Bell. She's had another vision of him.

I try to get back to sleep, but it turns into a night of turning and tossing. I can't stop thinking about bad luck. Is it bad luck that Skyler Dawkins had my number, but I didn't think to get hers? Is it bad luck that all of Skyler's social media accounts are private, which means we can't send her a message? I eventually fall asleep, not knowing if she'll agree to meet with us.

But when I wake up in the morning, there's a single text glinting up from my phone. Actually, there are twenty texts waiting for me. Nineteen of them are from the Courtyard Kids group chat, mostly involving a heated debate between Jeffrey and DeSean on the best dipping sauce at their favorite restaurant. I skim those before tapping the one text I have from an unmarked number.

Hey. It's Skyler. I had a weird dream. Text me when you know more about the . . . cookie incident.

I quickly text her back, asking if she wants to meet up with Mary and me. It's a mistake to get excited and think she'll respond immediately. I sit at the kitchen table, eating a bowl of cereal, checking my phone between bites. After a few disappointed minutes, though, I realize that Skyler sent her text at three in the morning. "Great. She's not going to be up for hours. . . ."

Mom loves to sleep in on Saturdays too. I'm sitting at the table, watching the light move across the patch of grass outside, when Grammy's bedroom door opens. My heart stops a little in my chest. My entire body goes still. But—of course—it's Mary who walks out of the shadows. I try not to let the disappointment show on my face. Sometimes the only thing I want in the entire world is to have Grammy walk out of that room again. I'd give anything for one more good morning, one more smile.

Mary yawns loudly, unaware of my thoughts. It looks like she didn't even sleep. I'm about to ask her about it when she sets a beautiful hourglass on the table in front of me. It's about the size of my thumb, with small engravings in the wood. As I watch, the grains trickle down, but slower than any hourglass I've seen. It's like they're moving one grain at a time.

"Doomsday countdown . . . ," she mumbles. "I'll explain. After coffee."

She crosses the room and starts fiddling with our coffee maker. It is a struggle to not ask all the questions I want to ask because I'm pretty sure she just casually used the phrase *doomsday countdown*. Instead, I listen to the *drip drip* as she makes her coffee. She opens the fridge, swirls in some creamer, and then stirs.

"You don't drink coffee, do you?" Mary asks.

I shake my head. "No."

"Good. It takes a *lot* of effort to get used to it. My gift was messed up for *weeks*. Coffee gives short boosts, followed by big crashes. I was seeing probabilities floating around everywhere. And then I'd crash so hard that I couldn't keep my eyes open in afternoon classes. Tea is a much safer alternative."

She takes the seat beside me. I can't hold the questions back any longer.

"Did you really just say *doomsday countdown*?!"

Mary nods. "Yes. See how slow it's moving? It was tricky to get the spell right. I attuned it to the exact time of your first vision. The one in the courtyard. Now you can see how much time has elapsed . . ." She points to the bottom of the hourglass. "Which means this gives you a rough estimate of how much time you have left."

Now she points to the top of the hourglass.

"I'd guess you're looking at about two more weeks until the point of no return. The only problem is that it can change. It's all based on probabilities. Right now, if all the most likely things happen, this is how long you have to save the day. But if something unexpected occurs? It could definitely accelerate the timeline. You'll have to keep an eye on this."

I glance up from the hourglass. "But this is yours? Isn't it?"

"You can borrow it," Mary says. "Grammy gave it to me as a gift. On the day of my first vision. She told me it was the perfect gift for her most punctual granddaughter."

We both smile at that. I can *almost* hear Grammy saying those words. Both of us instinctively look toward Grammy's room. The door is still open. All the emotions I've kept buried in the deepest corners of my heart start to rise again. I feel like I'm about to cry, so it's a relief when Mary speaks first.

"I miss her so much," Mary says. "You know she used to come up a lot when we were little. She'd spend the whole week with us in the mountains. Show us all the best trails, even though we were the ones who lived there. There was this one spot where we always took our shoes off and walked into the river. I miss her. . . . I started missing her even before we lost her."

I nod. "I know I got to be around her all the time. It's not fair for me to miss her, when I had so much more of her than you and Martha did. But it's almost like . . . I don't know. The spot where she was in my heart . . . It's just this big hole now. And nothing else seems to fit. I try not to think about it too much. It just makes me sad."

"Maybe nothing else is *supposed* to go there," Mary offers. "Maybe that's Grammy's spot and it always will be. I don't think there's anything wrong with keeping it that way."

For a second, neither one of us says anything. Mary sips her coffee. It makes her look so much older and wiser than me. The morning light finally angles through the window, pouring a faded gold across the table. I'm about to offer to make breakfast when my phone buzzes on the table. I swipe the screen and start reading:

Where can we meet? I have volleyball at 5pm. Any time before then!

I'm about to type in an answer when a second text buzzes through. I glance down to see that Skyler has shared her contact information, which includes an address. Mary's at my shoulder. She taps the link before I can. The map app takes over the screen. I'm assuming she wants us to pick a location that's close to her? I'm about to search for the nearest Starbucks when I realize her street looks familiar. I pinch my thumb and forefinger to zoom out.

"That looks like . . . the greenway."

A few quick swipes drag our view across the marked terrain. Sure enough, I swipe my way down to *home*. A small blue dot marks our current location. I tap that circle and ask for directions. The drive to Skyler's house is super roundabout, almost eighteen minutes away. But the walk? I swipe so that it converts the distances, then show Mary.

"She's literally a fifteen-minute walk down the greenway."

The greenway that Grammy and I would always walk. I eye Skyler's location again and know it's a spot we've passed before. Right between one of the dog parks and the bridge that almost always floods when it rains too much. We've passed Skyler's house before. A hundred times.

I text back: Meet at the dog park on the greenway? 30 minutes from now?

A few seconds pass, and I'm worried she's going to think I'm a stalker. But then I remember she's the one who sent her address to us. The text comes back.

Sure! I'll bring Bongo!

I reread her response a few times before frowning at Mary.

"Who is Bongo?"

She laughs. "You're a seer, and you can't figure that out? You asked her to meet you at a *dog* park, Celia. She's obviously bringing her dog."

I groan. "That's not what I meant! I wanted to meet *near* the dog park."

"Well, that's not what you texted."

"Do you think I'll have to go inside? I'm really not a dog person."

"Don't tell Bongo and his friends that."

We both laugh. I text back a final confirmation and then we get ready to leave. As I head upstairs, I catch a glimpse inside Grammy's room. Light is weaving through the shutters. The bed looks the same with that massive wooden headboard. A pair of matching lamps sit on flanking bedside tables. Grammy once told me that she thought they looked like trees bent by the wind, and I've never been able to see them any other way. Even her rocker still sits in the corner, but she's not sitting in it, sewing or reading or anything at all. I swallow the lump in my throat and head up to my room.

It's supposed to be chilly outside—and it's always colder on the shaded greenway—so I put on my most comfortable hoodie. I'm trying to stay focused, but my mind drifts back to the most recent coincidence. The same path Grammy and I walked, the place that was a refuge for both of us, just happens to lead to Skyler Dawkins's house? It's almost like Grammy planned it this way. I'm sure if I could ask her, she'd just smirk mysteriously back at me. Maybe she'd tell me that magic is all around us, happening all the time.

For the first time since her death, it feels like that's true again.

Twenty minutes later, I'm standing outside the dog park with my fists balled inside my sleeves, wondering if there are any heating spells in the guide book. It's colder than I thought it was. Mary's huddled near me for warmth. We watch as a small pack of dogs runs around inside the fence line. Every time their play brings them hurtling past the area where we're standing, I flinch a little, even with a fence between us.

I'm not afraid of dogs. But I'm not *not* afraid of dogs.

Mary nudges my shoulder. I look up and see Skyler Dawkins coming across the wooded bridge in the distance. The greenway's paved path curls from there to where we're waiting, and I can feel my heart pounding in my chest. What happens if she doesn't accept any of what we're about to tell her? What if she chooses Patrick over us? This could go a hundred different ways.

Skyler offers a wave. That's a good start. She's even prettier out here in the early sunlight. Her hair falls past her shoulders in naturally tight curls. She's wrapped up in one of those brightly colored, fuzzy jackets that are so popular now. Hers is an emerald-green color that matches her eyes.

I manage to wave back before seeing the massive creature that's marching at her side. Bongo is not a dog. He's a horse with canines. I'm surprised the puddles around us aren't shaking like that scene in *Jurassic Park*. He might look friendly, but he's literally an avalanche of white fur gliding straight toward me. I let out something that's half squeak and half yelp as he jumps up.

"Oh! Okay! Wow. Very friendly . . . wow. That's . . . wow, a lot of licking."

Skyler yanks on his leash, but she's probably half his size. I do my best to turn my body, shoving one hand out to keep him from jumping, but that just means he starts slobbering all over my fingers. "Sorry! He just gets really excited about the dog park. Come on. It'll be easier to talk once he's inside."

And with that, she marches straight toward the gates. There's no time to ask her if we can talk *outside* the fence. She's already got the entryway open. She barely manages to unclip Bongo before he goes thundering off. Three other dogs break from their play to come back and exchange sniffs. Is this bad luck? Being forced into a rendezvous inside the one place I'd rather not go?

I follow Mary inside and guide us to the nearest corner. I'm trying to stay far enough away from the dogs that none of them take any interest in me. Skyler glances over her shoulder, realizes we're not following her into the center of the park, and circles back to join us. All the other dog owners are standing near a set of covered tables about a hundred yards away.

"Right," Skyler says. "Forgot we'd need privacy."

I nod. "Yes. That's why we're over here. Privacy."

A retriever comes zipping past us, missing me by just a few steps. I have to resist jumping back over the fence as Mary introduces herself. "I'm Celia's cousin. Mary. I'm a seer too."

Skyler's eyes dart between us. There's so much eagerness in her expression. It reminds me of how we used to kink water hoses as kids, then watch as tons of water came pouring out all at once.

"So . . . there are more of you? You're like one big family? And is all of this . . . I don't know . . . Do you have the same magic? And do you seriously call it that? *Magic?* Do you tell people? Because this is so, so weird . . . no offense."

Mary and I exchange a grin. We thought our first conversation was going to be focused on convincing Skyler that she was—in fact—a seer. It sounds like she's already accepted that part.

"Slow down," Mary replies patiently. "This is all a lot. Especially if you didn't grow up in a family that talked about it. Can we ask you a few questions? About your family?"

Skyler nods. "Sure. Yeah. Is that important?"

"It might be," I say. "Were you born in Oklahoma?"

I'm expecting her eyes to shock wide. Maybe she'll think we used magic to figure it out, rather than learning about her birthplace from the Cleary Family Guide Book. But to our surprise, she shakes her head. "No. I was born here in North Carolina."

Well, that's unexpected. I think about the note in the family tree. The only person left unconfirmed was supposed to be about Skyler's age, but they were also born in Oklahoma. What does that mean? Was the note wrong? Or is Skyler from a completely different family?

Mary takes a new approach. "What about your grandmothers? Were either of them . . . odd?"

Skyler shrugs. "No idea. I never met them."

Another surprise. It also makes everything a lot trickier. If she's like us, her grandmother would have been magical.

She would have had premonitions in some form or another. But now there's no way of knowing. And it's not like we can just ask for her to bring us her most recent family tree. Some people are super private about that kind of thing.

"Let's focus on right now," I say. "You seem kind of . . . okay with the whole seer thing?"

Skyler shrugs again. I'm starting to get the sense that she's a pretty go-with-the-flow person.

"It makes sense, I guess."

Mary snorts. "It makes sense? Why does it make sense?"

"I don't know. I've always just had a sixth sense about stuff. And that conversation with Celia at the bakery had me thinking . . . I've been having these dreams . . ."

Her cheeks blush a violent shade of red.

"I didn't tell *anyone* because it's so embarrassing. But after we talked, I realized it was kind of weird. At least, I've never heard of dreams working like this. I dream about Patrick Bell pretty much *every* night. I've been dreaming about him for weeks. I just thought it was because I have a crush on him, you know? But that's *weird*, isn't it? To dream about someone *every* single night?"

"Not weird," Mary corrects. "And probably not just dreams. Those are called visions."

"And after each vision," I add, "you smell cookies, right?"

This time, Skyler's eyes do go wide. "Yes! At first, I thought it was just my clothes or something. The smell of the bakery on my jacket. But one time I woke up and it was like I was standing in the middle of the bakery, even though I didn't even work that weekend."

"Everyone has a scent when they see the future," Mary explains. "What were the visions?"

"I don't remember all of them. I just remember that they repeated a lot. I had one where Patrick was standing in front of me, smiling. I couldn't see anything else around him. He was wearing his basketball jersey, though. And he was really . . . sweaty. Not like a handsome sweaty either. Kind of a gross sweaty. Anyways. He lifted both arms. Kind of like he was pumping his fists. Celebrating something. I had that dream four nights in a row. I thought it was just because I was *imagining* him being happy."

A piece of the puzzle slides into place.

"You saw the game-winning shot," I say. "Or the celebration after, I guess."

Skyler nods. "I was in the crowd that night. Half the school was. I saw him put his arms up and it was like . . . an echo. Almost like I was the one who made it happen. But then the rest of the school mobbed him. That never happened in my dreams. I always thought he was smiling at *me*, but with all those people there, he . . . he just forgot I was there. He never even looked at me after the game."

Mary glances my way. One concern was that Skyler wouldn't want to confront Patrick. In an ideal world, we could reverse the spell without him knowing. But Mary thought it was a very real possibility that we'd have to actually talk to Patrick face-to-face. Maybe this is the crack in the armor that we needed. If Skyler thought Patrick had a crush on her, too, I'm sure she wouldn't want to ruin things by revealing any of this. But if she's been feeling abandoned by him? It's way more likely she'll agree to work with us.

I'm so deep in thought that I barely notice an old beagle sniffing its way along the fence line behind me. I jump a little when he grazes my foot, even though he looks harmless.

"Let us tell you what we know so far," Mary suggests. "And we'll see if it lines up with what you've experienced. How does that sound?"

Skyler nods. I'm glad Mary came. She sounds like our school counselor. She's very comforting. It takes about ten minutes for us to explain everything we know. Skyler looks like I looked when I was five years old, and Grammy first explained all of the magic to me. It's a wonder her head doesn't explode. I spend most of Mary's explanation dodging a playful husky that seems to think I'm his new best friend. At least Bongo doesn't come bounding up to renew his affections.

"So, Patrick is super lucky," Skyler concludes at the end. "And the rest of the eighth-grade class will be unlucky. And you think that's the way it will be for *the rest of their lives*?"

Mary and I both nod.

"Unless we stop it," I add.

"Wow," Skyler says. "I can't believe this. I messed everything up!"

Mary shakes her head. "No. Not true. How could you have possibly known? If no one ever told you about any of this? I'm sure there are other seers like you out there. People who didn't have their family helping them and teaching them the whole time. It's not your fault, but now you know the truth about what's going on. What you do *now* is what matters."

Mary sounds like a coach, giving some kind of halftime speech. And it's actually working. Skyler is nodding along. I remember she mentioned volleyball in her text earlier. Clearly, she's used to getting pumped up before big games. She looks like she's ready to climb mountains.

"Just tell me what to do."

"Step one," I say. "Please get Bongo off me."

Her monster of a dog has circled back and doesn't even have to jump to lick at my neck and face. I hold out both hands again until Skyler gets him to run off with the other dogs.

"Okay. What about step two?" Skyler asks.

"We need to go to the Spellbound Bakery."

CHAPTER SEVENTEEN

A Trail of Bad Luck

Sunday is all about finishing homework and finalizing plans.

I check my phone before coming downstairs. I know Jeffrey's still in Bethesda, Maryland, for a soccer tournament with his travel team. I've texted him a few times, but so far, he hasn't responded at all. It has me groaning about the mistake on the bus and again about getting caught following Patrick to class. I thought it wouldn't be a big deal, but I guess without an explanation, Jeffrey's left to his own imagination about what's going on. I'll have to wait until the bus stop on

Monday to make things right. I just hope I *can* make it right.

That morning, Mary and I both notice that the pace of the hourglass has slowed. It's just one grain every few hours or so. She thinks that's a good sign. The probabilities are factoring in our meeting with Skyler—and a successful rendezvous has increased our chances of stopping the doomsday. But the end of the weekend means that Mary's forced to pack up and hit the road. I apologize about how much homework she probably has piled up for Monday, but she says she's finished it all. Of course. My cousin never misses a step. I thank her with the biggest hug I can manage. She pulls me in close before getting in the car.

"Hey. Keep me updated. I'm two hours away. All it would take is a quick car ride. I ran all the probabilities again last night. It's hard to see much because you and Skyler are such wild cards, but the chance our plan works goes up a *lot* if Skyler gives this next step her all. Remind her that no boy is worth creating a doomsday. She has to put everything she can into the counterspell. Got it?"

I nod as she climbs into the front seat of her car.

"I'll text you. Promise."

"Don't forget to sleep. A well-rested seer . . ."

". . . is a seer who can see all that there is to see," I finish. It was one of Grammy's favorite sayings. "Thanks, Mary. I couldn't have done this without you."

"I bet you could have. You're amazing, Celia. Keep up the good work. Keep me posted."

She offers me a final wink, starts her car, and pulls off down the road. I watch until the brake lights vanish around a corner. Deep breaths. I take one after the next and remind myself that just because she's leaving doesn't mean I'm alone.

Mary's advice—her entire plan—is with me. Grammy's advice is always there too. That's the best part about family. You're never alone, not if you've taken the time to tuck them away in your head and your heart. Mary's visit reminded me of that. That space in my heart? Grammy's not gone from it. She's still there. Still smiling and whispering and encouraging.

I just have to be patient enough to keep listening.

✳   ✳   ✳

Monday arrives.

I feel prepared for the magical problems we're about to face, but I don't feel prepared *at all* for the Jeffrey dilemma. We still haven't talked. No phone calls. No texts. That's definitely not normal. Even if he was out of town, he almost always texts me funny things. I've spent most of the morning trying to figure out how to apologize to him. I didn't mean to hurt his feelings, but I doubt it was fun seeing Patrick's name written in my handwriting on some random worksheet.

As I walk up the street, he's already waiting at the bus stop. The Kapowski sisters are there too, but thankfully, they're standing all the way up by the stop sign. I take my place beside Jeffrey. A jumbled stack of words is waiting at the front of my brain, ready to topple over and come spilling out. I take a deep breath and begin.

"Hey, I'm—"

"Look, I just—"

We both cut off at the same time. The timing draws out smiles from each of us. It's like we're back at the beginning. Before we knew each other so well. Jeffrey recovers first.

"Sorry. Do you . . . do you want to go first? I'll go first? Yeah, I'll go first. So look . . . I'm *really* sorry. I spent all weekend feeling like such a noob. I know that you're doing your whole . . ." He waggles his fingers. "Obviously you wrote his name because you're . . . thinking about him because of the magic stuff? I know you don't like Patrick. Right? You don't like him? I mean, if you did, I'd totally understand. He's super cool. It's just . . . I thought . . . you and me . . ."

His shoulders hunch in slightly as he waits for my answer, and I realize he's been stuck on this question since seeing Patrick's name on my worksheet last Friday. I can't help laughing at how silly it is, even though I'm sure it doesn't feel silly to him. "Jeffrey. No. I obviously like *you*."

"Right, right, right . . ." He straightens his shoulders, standing a little taller. "I knew that. I just . . . I'm sorry. I was so distracted all weekend thinking about it. But I couldn't text you to tell you that I was sorry for storming off the bus. I jumped in the hotel pool with my phone in my pocket! It stopped working after that. I'm sorry if you . . . I mean, I don't know if you texted."

That's one mystery solved. "I texted a few times. It's good to know that you weren't just ignoring it."

"Of course not!" Jeffrey sputters out. "Trust me, I'd found several amazing sloth memes to send you as apologies. But my new phone won't be here until later this afternoon. I was going to use someone else's, but then I realized I don't have your number memorized. Won't make that mistake again. Anyways. I got you these. To say I'm sorry . . ."

I watch as he fishes through his bag. A second later, he reveals a box of my favorite chocolates. They're the ones that Grammy used to buy from a local chocolatier for Valentine's Day. We'd all sit on the couch, watching bad movies and taste-testing each flavor.

"But they, uh, they kind of melted . . ." Jeffrey explains.

Laughing, I open the box. Usually these chocolates are a work of art. Perfect shapes with clever designs on them. But Jeffrey's right. They definitely melted and then re-formed into something that looks more like a fourth grader's art project.

"They're just more abstract now," I say with a smile. "They're perfect. Thanks, Jeffrey. I'm sorry about the other day, too. Patrick is on my mind because something is happening at our school. Something big. But I promise you: he is *not* my type."

Jeffrey blushes a little because the implication behind those words is that Jeffrey *is* my type. I pluck out one of the chocolates, break it down the middle, and hand him one half. We try them at the exact same time.

"Coconut," he says, smacking his lips. "Aggressive amounts of coconut."

I laugh as the bus pulls around the corner. It feels good to have this part of my world set back the way it should be. It's like the one cloud hanging over my day—and over the plan with Skyler—has finally cleared out of my morning skies. I feel ready for what's next.

"So . . . how'd you do?" I ask as we board the bus. "In the tournament?"

He shrugs in response. I can't help frowning. Usually Jeffrey never passes up the chance to talk soccer. As we slide into our normal seats, I can tell something else is bothering him.

"Was the hotel fun at least?"

Jeffrey sighs. "Sorry. I'm still in a bad mood about the whole soccer thing. I lost us the tournament. The final game came down to penalty kicks. Coach always says to keep them low. I should have listened. My shot went off the crossbar. It was so unlucky. It's the first time I've lost us the game like that. Just not a good feeling, I guess."

Unlucky, I think. *There's a lot of that going around.* It's impossible to tell if Jeffrey really *was* unlucky. Is this an example of the curse starting to spread? Or was this normal good luck and bad luck? I'm sure soccer players miss penalty kicks all the time. Still, a nagging feeling pricks at the edges of my mind. It's not just the missed kick. He also ruined his phone. And his chocolates melted? That's three unlucky happenings in a row.

Maybe the impact of Patrick's good luck is starting to reach beyond the other two Patricks. The sad look on Jeffrey's face is just one more reason to make sure we put a stop to it.

Unthinking, I reach for his hand. I lift it up and kiss one of his knuckles.

"Hey. It's going to be okay."

And then I literally *freeze* because the bus around us is super quiet. I'm wondering if maybe it's a spell or something, until I realize the sudden silence is a *result* of the loud kiss sound that I just made. Jeffrey's eyes are darting from his hand to my lips and back again. I can tell he's thinking about kissing me, the way I've thought about kissing him for weeks. Which has me silently praying.

Please, do not kiss me on the bus. I do not want my first kiss to be on the #6.

I'm not sure if Jeffrey can read minds—or if he just senses everyone else on the bus watching us. He lowers our hands, lacing his fingers smoothly through mine.

"Maybe I should miss penalty kicks more often," he whispers.

I laugh at that. His mood shifts completely. I grin, thinking Grammy would call what I just did its own kind of magic. For exactly three minutes, all of my other concerns fade away. I'm not worried about my quiz in first period. I'm not freaking out about the Patrick Bell dilemma. I'm just a girl holding a boy's hand on the eighth row of the bus. And then our driver slams the brakes.

Everyone jolts forward a little. Katie West is actually thrown into the aisle. There are cries of surprise. We all crane our necks to get a look at what happened. The bus driver has to work hard to turn the wheel and get us around the reason why she slammed the brakes.

My heart sinks as we glide around two other buses. Both from our school. They were clearly in an accident. I can see the scrapes and dents on the back of the front one. All of the students are at the windows, looking down at their bus drivers arguing. My mind is racing, though.

More bad luck, and this is just the beginning.

Sometimes if you're not looking for something, you'd never notice it. That's the way the school day goes. I'm sure everyone else thinks that it's a normal day, but I know what's *supposed* to happen, which means I'm starting to see the trickles of bad luck everywhere.

In first period, Jonathan Russell's pants rip down the

middle. He has to go call his mom to bring him a backup pair. In second period, everyone realizes they studied the wrong section of the periodic table. There are groans up and down the rows as Mrs. Arthur passes out quizzes.

At lunch, DeSean spills a drink all over Sophie. Jeffrey announces that he stepped on gum. Little things keep popping up, and I'm the only one who can see the pattern. Bad luck is spreading.

The final bell can't ring soon enough.

I tell Jeffrey to head home without me, aiming straight for the rendezvous location instead. The first stage of our plan is set to begin. Skyler's waiting at the back doors of the school. She flags me down and we head to the crosswalk together.

"I've been doing what you said," Skyler whispers. "Keeping the same emotion in my head all day so that I can channel it later. It's really *hard*. You kind of forget how long a day is. Class after class after class. Focusing on one thing makes the day feel like it takes forever."

I smile at that. "True. Last year . . ."

But the words trail off. Only a few people know that I

saved Jeffrey's life over and over again. I was on the verge of telling Skyler all about that until I realized that only Mary, Martha, and Grammy really knew about what happened. Even Mom doesn't know—how connected it all was to Grammy's death. I'm quiet for a second, then realize that Skyler *is* one of us. And sometimes really inviting someone in means being vulnerable.

"Last year, I had a death vision."

Skyler's eyes widen. "No way."

I nod. "Jeffrey. My . . ."

". . . your boyfriend," Skyler finishes for me. "He's super cute, by the way."

"Oh. Right. Yeah. My boyfriend." I try to act like that's not totally weird to say out loud. "I saved his life about twenty times last year. Don't tell him. He doesn't know. I mean, he knows I saved his life a few times. But he kind of just thinks I got lucky? He hasn't really pieced it together."

"So, he doesn't know that you . . . see stuff."

"Oh, he knows about that. He just doesn't know that I saw him dying. I thought that was kind of depressing, I guess. I just told him that I knew he was in danger. That's all."

Skyler nods. "That's smart."

"Anyways. I brought that up because I know the feeling. I spent every day thinking about it last year. How could I save him this time? Sometimes it was like the day moved in slow motion. Just take some advice from me: Don't forget about the real world. It's not good if we dive so far into the magic world that we forget *this* world. The one where everyone else we know lives. A lot of my family has struggled with that over the years."

We've reached the parking lot. Spellbound Bakery is waiting on the corner.

"Thanks," Skyler says unexpectedly. "I really appreciate everything. All of your help. Can you imagine what would happen if I hadn't met you? I'd have spent my whole life with all these weird dreams and I'd have no idea why they were happening."

I smile back at her. It *is* nice, I realize. This is how it felt living with Grammy. I didn't realize how special it was to have normal conversations about my gift. I knew I missed that feeling, but Skyler is like a brand-new lifeline. One more person who understands. Not to mention she goes to the same school as me.

"I'm glad we found each other," I say. "I needed a friend who gets all of this."

Skyler blushes as we enter the bakery. That bright scent of cookies fills the air. Skyler's uncle Dave is behind the register, talking to a customer. Skyler signals for me to follow her into the back area of the bakery. She told me she's only allowed to work ten hours a week, an exception made for family businesses, but she loves that the job gives her extra money to spend on whatever she wants. I follow her to a central table, surrounded by ovens. Pots and pans are hanging from one wall. Skyler starts gathering ingredients.

"Here are the instructions Mary wrote out," I say, offering a slip of paper. "You'll make the cookies exactly like you normally do. All the same steps."

The plan is a clever one. It was Mary's idea. A lot of magic is about familiarity. Repetition and memory and comfort. Those are important to the seer. If we're going to look into the future, we need to do it with our feet set firmly on the ground of the present.

Counterspells are kind of like mirrors. The entry Mary found in the Cleary Family Guide Book had a lot of useful suggestions. We learned the counterspell should be cast in the same place as the original spell. It also helps if the person who cast it—Skyler—is the one to undo it. Last but not least, the spell should take on the same general form as the one that caused the curse. Translation: we need to bake a *bad luck cookie.*

I sit on a stool, watching Skyler turn on a mixing bowl. She dumps ingredients in and looks as practiced at all of this as a professional baker would. Patiently she mixes everything. When the mixer slows to a stop, she uses a spatula to free the dough from the sides of the bowl.

"Now what?"

"The new ingredient," I answer, reading Mary's notes. "All of your *bad luck* emotion needs to channel into that ingredient. She also said it helps if it's something you really don't like."

She scans the spice racks. "What about cayenne pepper?"

"Hmm. Maybe too far? Patrick has to actually eat the whole cookie."

"Good point," Skyler agrees, searching again. "Oh. I know. Everyone *loves* toffee, but I hate it. I really don't like how it sticks in your teeth. The texture is weird. I've never been a fan."

She removes a covered basket from the refrigerator. The caramel-colored flakes look delicious to me. "Okay. Don't hold back," I say, echoing Mary's advice. "You have to put all the bad luck that you can into this cookie. Remember, what we're doing won't actually hurt Patrick. It will just cut off the momentum of his good luck. We have to do enough to stop him. You can do this, Skyler."

She nods, takes a deep breath, and begins. I watch as she sprinkles the toffee all around the bowl. Her face is set in a determined look. The mixing begins. A loud whir. Skyler's concentration never breaks. I can sense her magic forming, invisible in the air. I take a few steps back, just in case some of that bad luck decides it wants to jump to me somehow. I have no idea if that's possible, but Grammy always said to do what you could to reduce the risk of the unexpected. Which means I'm standing half-hidden beside an oven unit when Skyler finally looks up.

"It worked," she says. "I think it worked."

"All right. Now you just have to make one perfect cookie. Well, one imperfect cookie."

She uses an industrial-size scooper. I watch as she sets the ball of dough down on the center of the tray. It looks absolutely delicious. Mom has always strongly preferred eating the dough, and I know she'd be scooping some out if she were here. Skyler already has the oven preheating, which means it's ready to bake. She slides the tray inside, sets a timer, and lets out a massive breath—like she just finished defusing a bomb. In a way, that's what she did.

"Next step: Patrick."

And we just have to hope the bad luck cookie is enough to stop him.

CHAPTER EIGHTEEN

The Point of No Return

I'm not sure if I've ever been this nervous in my life.

Last year, I had a lot on my plate. Saving Jeffrey's life over and over again. But all of that was on *my* shoulders. There's a certain comfort to knowing that something is in your hands. You have the ability to make sure things go right. For the first time, I'm not the one in control. It's Skyler Dawkins who's going to have to pull this one off.

I choose my seat in the bakery very strategically. It's not too far from any of the other tables, so I'll definitely be able to listen in on their conversation. I set out my homework, even though I know I'm way too distracted to do any of it. The scene will look more convincing if I'm studying.

Dave has vanished into the back to do some other work. Skyler's behind the counter now. We keep exchanging nervous glances until a small *ding* announces a customer. I sneak a glance, and I'm surprised to see Patrick Bell is by himself. I watch, expecting his teammates to come sprawling in behind him. The door remains shut, though. I count this as a stroke of luck in our favor. He's actually alone.

I catch a few snippets from their conversation. Skyler follows the plan. She tells Patrick to go take a seat. Before he turns, I slide my earbuds in. There's nothing playing, but I want to make sure I look very unavailable for conversation. I need him to stay focused on Skyler. It works.

Patrick takes the seat directly behind me. I can hear his chair scrape across the floor. He drums his fingers on the table, humming a song to himself. I can literally *feel* the magic aura of luck around him at this distance. It's like a whisper in the air. Something that tells me to talk to him, to like him. Good thing we're putting a stop to this. I can tell the spell is already way more powerful than it should be.

Skyler reappears. I can see her nervously biting her lip. She swipes a stray hair behind one ear, settles herself, and starts the walk across the room to Patrick. This is the moment we spent so long planning out. I sit completely still, listening to every word.

"Here you go. One delicious cookie."

There's the slightest clatter of a plate being set down on the table. I can envision Patrick's winning smile. His hand reaching out for that gooey, half-melted cookie.

Please let the counterspell be strong enough. Please, please, please . . .

"What are these? Right here . . ."

An alarm goes off in my head. Skyler's voice shakes a little.

"Oh! I just was trying a new recipe. That's toffee. It's kind of like a toffee and chocolate chip recipe. Everyone says it's amazing."

There's an awkward pause. I wish I was facing the other way. There's nothing I want more than to see what's happening. Why is he reacting so weirdly?

"Oh. Right. I mean, it looks really good."

Another awkward pause. And then I hear the slight scrape of the plate again.

"It's just those other cookies are my *favorite*," Patrick says. "I mean that. The best I've ever had in my life. And, I don't know, maybe I'm being superstitious . . . but I feel like those were my good luck cookies or whatever. I've been playing really well since that first day you made them. Is there any way I could get one of those?"

I realize the sound that I heard wasn't him pulling the plate *toward* him. He pushed it away. That's not good. Skyler is smart enough to improvise.

"These are pretty much *exactly* the same. Just one ingredient changed. How about you try it? And if you don't like it, I'll get started on making a batch of the other ones."

She sounds so convincing. I sit there, waiting for his response. There's a little *ring* from the door chime. Another customer is walking in. An older woman who heads straight for the display case with all the cakes. The bell sound fades in time for me to hear Patrick's response.

". . . can't break the tradition. This is really important. I don't know. It's been my favorite part of the day. Coming here. Eating the cookies you made me. Would you do that? For me?"

We didn't plan for this to happen. We spent a lot of time debating if the spell would be strong enough, but we never discussed what to do if he just didn't *want* the modified cookie. I doubt he really knows what's happening—but it's a classic case of how superstitious people can be. It makes them really stubborn, even if he's actually right about this. The cookies *are* the reason he's been lucky.

Skyler's clearly struggling to figure out what to say. The customer at the front of the store waves, trying to get her attention. She looks like she's picked out a cake she wants. Instinct tells me this isn't going to work. No matter what she says or does to convince him. We wanted him to eat the bad luck cookie without knowing what was going on. It would have been easiest that way, if things went back to normal and he was completely unaware that we'd broken his good luck streak.

But that's not going to happen.

I turn around. "I'll take it from here, Skyler."

The girl lets out a sigh of relief. She marches back toward the counter to help the other customer. There's no one else in the store. Patrick sits up a little straighter. He's clearly confused by my appearance. He does smile, recognizing me from the last time we talked. But there's something odd about me taking over the conversation. I can tell he's already on the defensive. The only thing to do is to dive straight into the deep end.

"You're right. You've had quite a lucky streak."

The magic around him flexes. I can't see it like I could the other day, when my scrying spell was still active. There's no golden glow, but the magic is there, invisible in the air, stronger than anything I've felt in my life. He smiles that winning smile and leans a little closer.

"No kidding. And running into you again? I'd say that's pretty lucky too."

I can't remember the last time I saw someone this comfortable with flirting. He's completely confident. Another smile appears, and his magic *pulses* up against me. It's trying to tug a smile out of me. It's whispering that I should fall head over heels for Patrick Bell because who *wouldn't* like someone like him? I have to grit my teeth to keep myself from falling into the trap.

This is just charm magic. I like Jeffrey Johnson. Not this kid.

"I'm not interested," I reply. "I am much more interested in your good luck, though. Two full-court, game-winning shots. I saw that first one. It looked like it was going to land way short, didn't it?"

Patrick falters a little. He's surprised, I think, because this is probably the first time someone has said anything negative to him in weeks.

"It didn't land short. It went in. I made the shot."

"Twice," I say. "What are the odds of that? And then those shoes you won. Pretty lucky. It's kind of unnatural, don't you think? This streak that you're on . . ."

He forces that smile back out. "My dad would say when it rains, it pours."

"I've heard that phrase. You're using it wrong, though. It means the opposite. When one *bad* thing happens, everything seems to go wrong. And that *is* what's happening. To everyone but you."

The expression on his face changes. Before, he was slightly unsure of what was happening. Maybe he thought I was actually flirting with him. It's clear now, though, that we're talking about something more serious. It has him back on the defensive.

"I don't know what you're talking about."

"You've been getting lucky because of the cookies," I explain. "Those cookies that Skyler has been making you. I know it sounds ridiculous, but they really were good luck charms. The problem is that you got too much. That's why everything has been going right all of a sudden. . . ."

He shakes his head. "No—no way. I've just been practicing a lot . . ."

"And that explains making two full-court shots? Or winning those shoes? I'm sure there are a thousand other things that have gone right for you in the past few weeks. Do me a favor. Name *one* bad thing that's happened to you recently."

He shakes his head again, but I can tell the challenge has stumped him. Nothing bad has happened to him because right now, he's got so much good luck swirling around him that nothing bad *can* happen to him.

"I really don't know what you're talking about. . . ."

"Then why are you here? Why did you demand that specific cookie?"

This time he's trapped by his own words. He already said they were his good luck charms.

"I wasn't being serious," he answers. "Cookies can't *actually* make you lucky."

But we both hear the truth in his voice. He doesn't believe his own words. He really thinks—in some weird way he can't explain—that his good luck started in this bakery. He's right.

"Do you want to know what's really happening or not?"

He takes a deep breath. "Sure. Whatever."

"Okay. Here's the truth: Skyler was shoving doses of good luck into those cookies without knowing it. You had a bad day. She felt bad for you, so she made that first cookie.

It was literally a *lucky* cookie. And you came back every day to get more. The only problem is that she made you way *too* lucky. Skyler didn't realize what she was doing because she's new to all of this. No one is supposed to have that much luck. It creates an imbalance in the rest of the world."

He shakes his head. "That's ridiculous . . ."

Again, I can hear the thread of doubt in his voice. He *knows* exactly how lucky he's been. None of what's been happening to him is normal. Not when you take a step back and look at the whole picture. I know he knows that.

"The world always tries to balance itself out," I say. "That's the problem. You're so lucky that everyone else around you is starting to get unlucky. The first people who experienced it were Patrick Adams and Patrick Connors."

He frowns, but I can tell I've got his attention.

"You all have the same name and go to the same school. Skyler's magic accidentally connected the three of you. Patrick Adams? His prize robot blew up in the middle of a competition. Patrick Connors broke his arm, and then his family was in a car accident. No one was hurt, thankfully, but that was this time. Who knows what might happen next time? I know you didn't mean for this to happen, but you're making them unlucky.

"And it's only going to get worse, Patrick. I know magic. It's my whole life. If we don't stop what's happening right now, the entire eighth grade will be cursed. You'll be fine. Better than fine. You'll always make those half-court shots and win things. But everyone else around you? The rest of us won't have any luck at all. We'll live horrible lives where nothing goes right. It's already started."

I can tell he's trying to process all of this. It probably still sounds absurd.

"I don't believe you."

"Two school buses collided this morning. Bad luck," I answer. "I've seen a dozen other cases of bad luck just today. And those things—people spilling drinks or studying the wrong chapter for homework—they're just the beginning. Pretty soon we'll be the most miserable eighth graders in the history of the world. Well, all of us except for *you*."

His eyes fall. At first, I think he's ashamed. But then I

realize he's looking at the cookie that's sitting on the table between us. I spy the little bits of toffee poking out of the melted dough.

"Why did Skyler change the cookie?" he asks.

"That cookie is a counterspell," I say. "The magic is growing out of control, but that cookie will stop everything before it's too late. You can save all of us, Patrick. All the misery that's about to happen. For the rest of our lives. Eat that cookie, and it stops."

He reaches out and pulls the plate closer to his side of the table. I watch as he lifts the cookie delicately in one hand. It's cooled down, just firm enough now that it doesn't break apart.

"I have to eat the whole thing?"

I nod. "The whole thing."

"And if I eat this, what happens to me? Won't I be unlucky?"

I shake my head. "No. You've got so much good luck that this will just balance it back out. All that will happen is you'll go back to normal. Everything will be the way that it was."

"No more half-court shots?"

I shrug. "Only the ones you make with your own skill and hard work."

Patrick lifts the cookie to his lips. Our eyes lock and I can tell he really believes me. It's like a missing puzzle piece has clicked into place. Maybe he didn't understand why things had suddenly gotten so much better in his life—but now he has the answer. A weight falls off my chest as he opens his mouth to take a bite.

But then he busts out laughing. I watch in horror as he reaches out and deliberately drops the cookie onto the ground. It lands with a sickly *splat*. He shakes his head at me.

"Good luck cookies? That's so ridiculous." He leans in and lowers his voice. "But just in case you *are* telling the truth . . . why would I ever eat a cookie that takes this away? My life has been so amazing. I was alone. For the entire first semester, no one even talked to me. No one really cared about me. But now? Everyone knows the name *Patrick Bell*. Everyone."

I watch as he takes a napkin. A small dash of chocolate splattered onto his new shoes. He wipes the spot, and it comes away looking even cleaner than before somehow. He stands up.

"You can't do this," I whisper, begging him now. "Please, Patrick. You'll ruin everyone else's lives. This could put all of us in serious danger. People *will* get hurt."

"It's not my fault that things are happening to other people." He sounds like he's trying to convince himself that that's true. "Honestly, it kind of sounds like you're just jealous of me."

And with that, he steps over the bad luck cookie that's splattered on the ground. Skyler walks over to say something, but he just waves her off. We're both helpless as we watch him walk out the door. The chime rings, and then he's gone.

"Now what?" Skyler asks.

For the first time, I don't have an answer.

CHAPTER NINETEEN

The Consequences

As soon as Patrick leaves, customers start showing up. A *lot* of customers.

More than I've seen in my two visits to the Spellbound Bakery combined. It feels like peculiar timing. Good business for them, but it also means that Skyler and I have no time to discuss next steps. I decide to call my mom for a ride home, only to discover my phone is dead. Which is also weird. I'm pretty sure it was fully charged at the end of the school day. How on earth did it die so fast? As Skyler tackles the long line of customers, I reach under the table to plug in my charger. But no matter how

I jiggle or adjust the cord, the light won't blink back on.

"Great."

It isn't too far or too late to walk home. I glance outside. At least the weather is nice. I wave one final time to Skyler—who is whipping around behind the counter, trying to serve food to the flood of customers. She offers a distracted wave back. I can tell her mind is still on Patrick and everything that just happened.

At least I'm not alone, I think. *I have someone to help me through all this mess.*

I still can't fully believe what Patrick did. It would have made perfect sense to me if he didn't believe me. Magic is always hard to believe at first. But Patrick chose to not eat the cookie. Faced with his own good fortune versus the rest of the eighth grade, he actually picked himself. It was the most selfish thing I've seen someone do since Wes Bearden ate Connie Wong's entire birthday cake back in third grade when no one else was looking. And that didn't have nearly the same level of consequences.

I'm about halfway home—lost in thought—when the clouds roll in.

The rain starts a minute later. Of course I don't have a jacket. I do my best to take the streets that have more tree cover, sprinting whenever I'm completely exposed. At one point, a passing car splashes a muddy puddle, soaking my socks and shoes. The bad luck spreading from Patrick seems like it's personally targeting me. Maybe it is.

"Because I'm the one who he'll think of as his enemy now . . ."

I was half hoping that thought would pump me up a little. Steady me so that I could face the challenge ahead. Instead, it starts raining even harder. By the time I enter the passcode for our garage, I'm soaked to the bone. Mom is in her room. From the sound of it, she's on the Peloton racing in some kind of hypno–Tour de France. I slip inside my room and close the door.

There's a backup charger by my bedside table. I plug my phone in, change into some warm clothes, and pace restlessly around the room. I can either start my homework or start researching in the family guide book. I take a deep breath. Homework first. I need time to think and process.

Some mindless worksheets might do the trick.

But when I start to unzip my bag, I realize that it's been unzipped for the *entire* walk home. Water sloshes along the bottom. Every notebook, every binder, completely soaked.

"Seriously? How could this get any worse?"

I stand up, trying not to think bad thoughts about Patrick Bell. As I cross the room, my phone buzzes back to life. There's a text from Mary: How did it go?

Not good. Patrick turned down the bad luck cookie. He wants to keep his good luck!

The phone rings immediately.

"Mary?"

"Hey, Celia. I thought that might happen. There was a very high probability that he'd find the altered cookie strange. I was really hoping he would decide to eat it anyways. After all, most people think superstition and good luck aren't real. They're embarrassed to be caught believing in even the smallest magics. How did it end?"

I sighed. "He dropped the cookie on the floor and told me he planned on keeping the good luck. He pretended like he didn't believe what we were saying, but I'm pretty sure he did. I think he knows the truth and he's choosing his own good luck over everyone else."

"That's so selfish. But people are selfish. And besides, that wasn't our *only* strategy."

"Wait. It wasn't?"

I can imagine Mary smiling on the other end of the phone.

"Of course not. I didn't want to mention the other plan because it would have kept us from focusing on the first option. There's one other thing you can do. Turn to page seventy-three. I dog-eared it . . ."

"You dog-eared it? Grammy would ground you for that."

Mary laughs. "I know she would. Basically, there's one other way to *reduce* luck. It's called a Critical Opposition Override. The example in the book isn't about good luck and bad luck. I'm pretty sure it focuses on something else . . ."

"Minimizing a seer's magic?"

Mary is quiet for a second. "Yeah. Pretty sure that's what it was about. Can't remember."

Which is a lie because Mary's mind is a steel trap. She

doesn't forget anything. I realize she knows about this section because she read it sometime before last weekend. I know Mary's always struggled with her gift. It was hard for in high school to keep her gifted thoughts quiet. I also know that madness is a fear that every seer in our family experiences, knowing how many family members couldn't bear the burden of their own incredible gifts. To know too much meant having too much weight on their shoulders. It sounds like Mary was trying to find a way to reduce her own gift.

"Okay. How does it apply to this situation?"

"The same principles should work. It's a shock to the system. Right now, he's smothered in good luck, right? The magic is basically force-feeding him good things. If you can create a real-life situation, though, where the *opposite* happens, it shocks the system because his mind has been rewired now to expect good things to happen. Especially after your conversation."

I'm half listening and half scanning the page that she flagged.

"I'm not sure I get it. What do I have to actually do?"

Mary takes another deep breath. "You have to embarrass him."

"Embarrass him? That's it?"

"It has to be something big, Celia. Have you looked at your hourglass?"

I let out a groan. The hourglass! I haven't looked at it in a couple of days because I forgot what Mary said about it changing depending on what happened with Patrick. It's at the bottom of my book bag, a little wet from the rain, but as I hold it up to the light . . .

"Oh . . ."

"How much is left?"

"It's already at the halfway point! And the sand . . ." I eye it for a second, just to make sure I'm not seeing things. "It's moving *way* faster. Not one grain at a time anymore. This is a clear trickle now."

"You're heading for the point of no return," Mary confirms. "We went for a home run. That was our big chance. But now Patrick is onto you. And he knows Skyler tried to sabotage him too. That's why the timer is moving faster. The two most likely people to stop him are on his radar. It will be a lot harder to trick him if he's avoiding you both. And all of that good luck he's got? It's just going to keep building and building. Based on all my calculations, I'd guess you have . . . three days. Four if you're lucky, but we both know you won't be."

It sounds hopeless, but Grammy taught me to never lose hope.

"What do I do? You said I have to embarrass him?"

"Yes, but it has to be one massive embarrassment. It's like in those old stories, where the person drives their spear through the one weak point in the dragon's armor. If you can pull this off, it might be enough to shatter all the good luck around him. Which means we're not talking about just tripping him as he steps off the bus. It needs to be big enough to match all the good luck he's already got. Do you understand?"

My mind is whipping through potential strategies, fed by all of my own nightmares about being embarrassed in front of my classmates, when the doorbell rings. "Let me call you back, Mary."

The music in Mom's room is too loud for her to hear

that someone's at the door. I start down the stairs, my mind still racing. It will have to be somewhere with a big crowd. Maybe a pep rally would work? I've got to figure something out as soon as humanly possible. A glance through the side pane shows Jeffrey's waiting on my stoop. I open the door.

"Hey, I'm glad you're—"

"I just wanted to—"

It's just like at the bus stop. Our words tangle, and we end up smiling like fools at each other.

"You go first," I say. It takes a second to notice that he's got items clutched in each hand. In his right, a piece of crumpled paper. In his left, a random string is dangling down.

"Okay. I came here to ask you to the dance. I had this whole plan to make it really special. I was going to write it on the back of the bus seat where we always sit together. I even bought these special markers that erase really easily." He shrugs, like that isn't the sweetest thing ever. "But you missed the bus in the afternoon three days in a row now! So I came up with a new plan."

He holds out the random string. I frown in confusion.

"Are you going to tie me up? Is this a kidnapping?"

He busts out laughing. "What? No! These were balloons! I bought you a bunch of balloons. As I walked over here, I don't know what happened! They must have slipped off the string when I wasn't paying attention? Look."

I follow him as he backs up a few steps. Sure enough, there's a distant herd of red and white balloons slowly making their way over the trees and to the next neighborhood. *More bad luck,* I think. Jeffrey lets out a sigh.

"I promise I tried to make it fun. But I'm out of ideas now. Will you—"

I cut him off with a huge hug. It jolts the breath from him.

"Yes, I'll go with you to the dance."

He's surprised for a second, then returns the hug. We don't break away as quickly as we usually would. At school, there's always that awkward feeling that someone might turn toward us at the slightest physical touch and shout, "Look! Jeffrey and Celia are holding hands!" I'm not sure why that seems so embarrassing, but it's always . . .

My mind connects the dots.

"Embarrassing. Lots of people. Let me see that flyer."

I snatch the sheet from him. It was designed by the year-book club. I can tell because DeSean does all the graphics for them. It has his signature look to it. At the top, the bold letters read: THE ANNUAL GET-DOWN DANCE. I glance through the details and see another coincidence. The dance is *exactly* three days from now. It lines up perfectly with the hourglass and the doomsday timeline. One final chance.

I've never heard it called the "Get-Down Dance," but I know this is the one dance that happens every year. Avery dragged me there when I was in sixth grade. It was fun for the first fifteen minutes, and pretty miserable for the next two hours. Kind of like someone had bottled up the most awkward parts of middle school and unleashed them in one big ballroom. I still have nightmares about how much cologne was swirling in the air. But I know one thing: the entire school was there.

"This is it!" I hug Jeffrey again. "This is how we beat him!"

Jeffrey smiles down at me. "Right. Wait. What?"

I smile at the puzzled expression on his face.

"Come inside. I'll explain."

CHAPTER TWENTY

Motivation

Three days.

I have three days to make a plan for the dance. As the clock starts to tick down, I feel like I'll be lucky to *survive* the coming days, let alone think up some amazing strategy for when the day of the dance actually arrives. The main problem is that Patrick's good luck is spreading—which means everyone else's bad luck is also spreading.

Later that night, Mom is watching the news when a familiar voice echoes from the speaker. Mom nudges me. "Isn't that one of your classmates?"

The interviewer walks us through a heroic tale. Apparently, Patrick rescued someone from drowning in one of the neighborhood pools. He just happened to be walking by when they fell in. The reporter calls him a local hero who was at the right place at the right time.

"I'll bet he was," I mutter under my breath.

It's obviously a good thing he saved someone's life. I'm not complaining about that. But I can't help wondering if the person who fell in was another eighth grader. Was it the shifting balances of luck that caused the accident, and forced Patrick to look like a hero, even though he's the one who caused it in the first place? The interview ends with Patrick smiling that winning smile at the camera. It almost feels like he's looking right through the screen, taunting me.

The next morning at school, he's featured on the announcements. He scored a record-setting forty-nine points in last night's game. There's no mention of the fact that they lost the game, or that the rest of the team didn't make a single shot. Another sign that his good luck comes with a clear cost.

As his good luck blossoms out, bad luck spreads like an overgrown plant. It snakes through the cracks of the rest of our lives, bursting out in unexpected ways. The worst of it happens whenever Patrick is flexing his good luck.

While he set records at the basketball game, DeSean was searching the woods behind his house for their dog. Wind blew the gate open on their back fence. DeSean even twisted his ankle before Tatyana spotted Slug the Pug rolling in the mud near Buoy Creek. And that morning, while Patrick was interviewed on the announcements, I set my sleeve on fire in our science class.

At lunch, Jeffrey reports an embarrassing incident with a toilet, refusing to share any more details. But it's Sophie's bad luck that takes the cake. We're all in the courtyard, hanging out like usual, when the drainage grate she's standing on gives way. She plummets six feet, releasing more curse words than I've ever heard one person use in a five-second stretch.

We all rush over to help her. Thankfully, she's not hurt. The janitor arrives a few minutes later to inspect the scene, and he announces that the bolts have been rusting away for years. Apparently, they chose that exact moment to stop working. I know it's not a coincidence, though. Just more bad luck. The janitor announces that the courtyard will be closed for a few days.

Patrick is ruining everything.

It's not just us, either. The school is full of mishaps that afternoon. People slipping in hallways. Paints exploding in art classes. One particularly unlucky kid—Wes Bearden— manages to glue himself to a desk. I'm not sure if that one is a case of bad luck, or just the status quo for him. Either way, the wave of incidents has me working double to come up with a good plan.

As the school day ends, I find myself bracing for impact. What's next? A flat tire on our bus ride home? Stepping on a piece of gum? The hallways are crowded as everyone makes their way to the buses. I'm following the flow of traffic when I hear something *shatter*.

It sounds like glass? No one else notices. There's a ton of noise and bustle, and I think the only reason I hear the noise is because I'm already on edge, expecting the worst.

When it sounds again, I follow the noise into one of the nearest science classrooms. Mrs. Heathers isn't at her desk. The room looks empty until I spot one person at the back, standing by one of the lab tables. I watch in shock as they raise a glass beaker above their head and bring it smashing to the ground. Glass scatters across the floor. There are two other beakers already broken in the growing pile at their feet.

"Patrick?"

His head whips in my direction. It's Patrick Adams. His chest is heaving. His brown eyes are wide. At the sight of me, he shrinks slightly back into his hoodie. Almost like he thought he was invisible until this very moment. Maybe that's how he always feels: invisible. He's got another beaker clutched in his hands and looks ready to smash it just like he did with the others.

I cross the room. He doesn't know me. Not really. But I walk up to him with as much care and concern as I can. I reach for the beaker, and he lets me have it. His hands are trembling. I set the glass down on the nearest table. A glance shows the skin beneath his eyes is a slightly darker brown. Like he hasn't slept much lately. Instinctively I reach out for his hand. The way Grammy used to when I was upset. He lets me lead him over to the nearest desk.

"Take a few deep breaths, okay?"

His eyes are locked on mine. He nods, breathing in deeply. As he sits there, I walk over to get the broom from the corner closet. I take a look at the blast radius and start at the outer edges, sweeping the glass into a large central pile. Patrick keeps taking deep breaths. I can tell he's recovering, slowly but surely.

"Want to talk about it?"

He shakes his head. I don't push him. I just keep sweeping up the mess, and after about thirty seconds, he decides to speak. His voice is a little deeper than most of the kids our age. It's only a surprise because it's changed a lot from the YouTube videos I watched.

"I'll clean it up. You don't have to do that."

"I know. I've got it, though."

He's quiet for a second. Then, "I don't know what happened. I just got so mad."

"About what?"

When I glance over, he's looking down at his own hands, like the answers might be written there in the dark lines of his palms.

"Nothing works. I don't get it. First, my robot exploded. The circuits overloaded. And there's just no *way* that happened. I spent hours on it. I made sure everything was perfect. There's no reason why it should have happened."

He shakes his head again, like he's trying to wake up from a nightmare.

"And then I was doing an experiment last period. No matter what I did, the chemicals wouldn't mix together the right way. I stayed after the bell. I tried to figure it out. It should work. I did it right. I followed all the steps. But it *didn't* work."

His chest is heaving a little again. I gesture with my hands. A motion that says *Take it easy, keep breathing.* He nods in response. I keep sweeping the glass up. This is the most I've ever heard him talk by a mile. Grammy taught me once that sometimes people just need to hear their thoughts out loud. Sometimes they don't need you to try to offer up a solution or wisdom or anything. They just need their voice to be heard. Which is why I stay quiet as he keeps going.

"I like science a lot. It makes sense. If you do this, then *that* happens. It's my favorite subject. It's logical." He gestures to the broken glass. "The rest of my life . . . I don't know. I don't have any control over anything else. Everything just happens *to* me. But with science, I know what to do. I get to be the one who *causes* things to happen. For some reason, even science doesn't work this week. Things that should happen aren't happening . . ."

He trails off. Maybe he realizes he's rambling. I see the way he's tempted to duck back into his hoodie and vanish. I speak before he can. "I get it, Patrick. It's okay to be upset."

"Sorry for breaking that stuff. I'm going to get in so much trouble. And sorry you had to clean it up. I'll take care of the rest of it."

He stands up, far steadier on his feet now. When he

reaches for the broom, I let him have it. But I keep hold of it long enough that he has to look me in the eye. I know I can't tell Patrick what's actually happening. I can't tell him why the thing he loves the most in his life doesn't make sense right now. Instead, I make a promise that I hope I can keep. It feels like I'm making the promise to him—and to Patrick Connors—and to the rest of the eighth grade. It's a promise for everyone.

"It's going to get better. This has been a weird week. But I promise you, it will get better."

He nods. "Thanks. It's Celia, right?"

"Celia Cleary."

He smiles once before turning to sweep the pile. He's really thorough about it. I can tell he's a scientist at heart because he scans the entire room for stray glass specks. He even gets down on hands and knees, inspecting the hidden edge of the room with meticulous care. That's when Mrs. Heathers returns. She sees the broken beakers and her eyebrows knit together. I realize Patrick's day is about to get a lot worse. But I also know he doesn't deserve any of this.

"It was my fault, Mrs. Heathers," I say quickly. "I wanted Patrick to show me something that I missed in my other class, and I forgot I had my backpack on. Knocked the beakers right off the counter. I'm so sorry. I'm late for my bus, so Patrick offered to finish cleaning it all up for me."

Mrs. Heathers sighs. "It's okay. How about you see me for lunch tomorrow? Help me clean and polish the *rest* of the beakers. Does that sound fair?"

I nod to her. "It does."

Before I leave the room, I glance back at Patrick. He nods a silent thank-you before bending back over the pile we swept. As I head for the bus, I hope beyond hope that my promise isn't an empty one. I hope I can actually turn all of this around. We have to figure out a way because Patrick Adams doesn't deserve a life filled with moments like this. Moments where nothing seems to work.

And it won't just be him. Every single one of us will tiptoe through the rest of our lives, hoping things don't go wrong, and getting used to the fact that they always do. I'll know the truth. Skyler will know and my friends, too. But everyone else? Friends and family will call them unlucky. Really superstitious people will think they're cursed. And they'll always say it with a little half smile, not fully believing it, and not knowing there was one person who caused it all.

Patrick Bell *has* to be stopped.

CHAPTER TWENTY-ONE

My Team

Grammy left 312 notes in the Cleary Family Guide Book. I know because I've read every single one of them. Counted them like stars in a sky that only I'll ever get to see. Like all the Clearys who came before her, she knew that knowledge wasn't something you came up with on your own. It's something built up over generations, seasoned by the trials and errors of those who came before us, and by those still to come.

My favorite note of hers is at the back of the book. I've read it a dozen times now. I can imagine her sitting in her rocking chair—the night before the field trip and her own sacrificial death—making one final note in that steady handwriting.

The original text reads: *Secrecy is a crucial component to the life of a seer. The nature of our craft demands privacy, denies friendship, and depends upon our ability to remain separate from the world.* It goes on like that for a while, preaching the code of distance to every seer who read this book over the years. The original writer suggests it might be feasible for a single loved one to know and keep your secrets as a seer, but that trusting them with such information could lead to every imaginable disaster.

Grammy's comment counters it in the margins: *I have found the opposite to be true.*

That note is why I've invited my whole team over tonight. I've reached a point of desperation. The only way to stop this doomsday scenario is if all of us work together.

It was one thing to give them each a glimpse of my secret. Avery watched me do a scrying spell. Jeffrey knows I get visions of what's going to happen. Sophie and DeSean both helped me save Jeffrey's life last year, so they know about it too. But it feels like an entirely new thing to invite them all over for a strategy session where my magic is the centerpiece of our plan. What if they decide that I'm really weird, once they know the whole story?

The first person to arrive is Jeffrey. He's breathing heavily. That doesn't stop him from pulling me into a one-armed hug. "Sorry . . . just . . . got . . . chased."

"Chased?"

He nods, still breathless. "Mr. Bowman's dog. Went right through the electric fence."

I don't like dogs, but I've always thought Mr. Bowman's was cute. I've also walked by their fence a hundred times without getting barked at. "Isn't it a little dachshund?"

"Yeah. So? Those things have vicious little teeth."

"I mean, it's the size of a toaster."

"A toaster with lots of teeth. These ankles are my moneymakers."

I glance at his ankles. "If it helps, I don't think your ankles are even in the top ten of all of your physical qualities. . . ."

It happens again. I realize, a second too late, what I'm actually saying. I basically just told him that I like the way he looks. A lot. My words have his cheeks glowing red. I blush with equal intensity, and I'm grateful when another knock interrupts.

Skyler Dawkins is on the porch. She's got her curly hair pinned up. I see the way she peeks around the room, and it's like a gut shot to realize she has the same look that all of Grammy's clients once had. She's searching for crystal balls and bewitched brooms. I smile when she realizes it's the most normal-looking living room and kitchen in the world.

"Huh." She spots Jeffrey. "You must be Celia's boyfriend."

He starts to open his mouth to introduce himself. But then he just nods, like he's been waiting for someone to pin a badge with that title on his chest for a while. I grin at his reaction.

"My name is Skyler Dawkins. I'm . . ."

Her eyes flick over in my direction. This is all new to her. She's probably not sure who she's allowed to talk to about her gifts. Jeffrey solves her dilemma by wiggling his fingers in the air.

"You do magic too? Cool. I'm normal. Celia keeps me around for my soccer skills."

"Normal is a stretch," I reply.

That earns a laugh from her, and just like that, we're all friends. Jeffrey heads over to the pantry. He pulls out various snacks and sets them on the center of the table. I forgot that I'm hosting people, and that hosts usually offer things like food. Thankfully, he's got me covered.

It doesn't take long for everyone else to arrive. Mary's car pulls into the driveway. She had the longest trip. I told her to call in over the phone, but she insisted on being here in person. Tatyana parks her sleek ride out front and joins DeSean as they march across the fresh-cut grass. Sophie's mom drops her off a few minutes later, and Avery is the last one to arrive.

Everyone comes with a story, a reason why they're late. And the stories all match Jeffrey's bad luck on the way here. DeSean couldn't get the garage door closed, and he had to go back inside to tell his dad it wasn't working. Tatyana rolls her eyes because I know she's not in the habit of being late to anything. Skyler's mom took the wrong entrance into the neighborhood and almost dropped her off at the wrong house. Sophie literally couldn't find her left shoe and had to throw on a pair of really old sneakers from the closet. And it all connects back to Patrick Bell.

"All right. Who has been experiencing a *lot* of bad luck?"

All of the eighth graders raise their hands: Desean, Jeffrey, Skyler, and Sophie. I put mine up as well. Avery doesn't lift her hand. Mary is busy taking notes. Tatyana looks like she's still trying to figure out why she was invited in the first place.

"There's a reason for that bad luck," I say. "Meet Skyler Dawkins."

Skyler waves. Avery snorts a laugh. "Wow. That's harsh, Celia. You're blaming all your bad luck on her? Not exactly a warm welcome to the group, is it?"

"But she's right. It really is my fault," Skyler answers. "I'm the one who started the curse."

That gets everyone's attention. I can see raised eyebrows around the room. The word *curse* has that effect. I'm about to defend Skyler—I feel the need to defend her—when Mary cuts in.

"How about we sit in the living room and talk? Instead of standing by the door?"

"Oh," I say. "Right. Yeah. Grab any snacks or drinks you want, then meet . . . over here."

It takes hearing Mary's words to realize I never welcomed everyone inside. We were just kind of standing awkwardly in the entryway. Everyone moves at the same time. Jeffrey starts pouring waters for people. Tatyana makes small talk with Mary as they grab a few snacks. The crew wanders into the living room, claiming cushions and chairs and couches. I pour myself a glass of water and can't help feeling super nervous. I can barely survive school presentations. Now I'm leading a meeting about my own hidden superpowers? I'm sure this is going to go perfectly.

Jeffrey appears at my side. "Hey. You've got this."

And then he heads over to join the others without another word. His confidence quietly becomes my confidence. I follow him. At the center of the living room, I've already set up an old art easel that I found in our garage. I take my place beside it and dive right in.

"Most of you know that I'm different . . . even though you might not know exactly *how* different I am. My family . . .

is a family of seers. You've probably heard a lot of different words for us: prophets, clairvoyants, witches. My family tree is full of people who, for better or worse, could see the future. I inherited their gifts. I can see glimpses of what's coming. And Skyler is a seer too."

She's watching a little wide-eyed from the couch. She offers a wave, maybe to remind everyone that she is the Skyler in question. I smile before continuing.

"She didn't know about her powers, though. My—" A lump forms in my throat. I have to tighten my jaw and steady myself. I remind myself that she's never fully gone, not as long as I hold on to her words and all the wisdom she offered me. "Grammy taught me about my gift because her grandmother taught her, and so on and so on. Skyler said the curse started with her. It did. But it's not really her fault. She didn't know what she was doing. She didn't even know she had a gift. All she wanted to do was help someone."

Jeffrey raises his hand. I roll my eyes.

"You don't have to raise your hand."

He shrugs. "So there really is a curse?"

"Yes."

He raises his hand again.

"What is it, Jeffrey?"

"Is this anything like *Agent Zero: The Curse of Time*? That's the one with the ships that can sail into space?"

DeSean adds, "That movie was *awesome*."

"No more questions for you," I reply. "Focus. No, it's not like . . . whatever that movie is. Skyler is a Charmist. Which means she can give little good-luck nudges. In this case, she was giving someone good luck cookies. The problem is that luck *multiplies*. Every time she gave this person a cookie, his luck grew more and more. The other problem is that luck works on a universal, balancing scale. If one person gets luckier, someone else has to lose their luck to even things out. . . ."

"Was the person DeSean?" Tatyana asks. "I *knew* there was something sketchy about how fast your follower count was growing."

DeSean makes a face. "I don't even eat cookies! I don't like them."

"You don't like cookies?" Jeffrey repeats. "What's wrong with you?"

"Hey! Focus! It's not DeSean. He just raised his hand because he's been unlucky lately, remember? His dog escaped the other day. His garage door wouldn't close right before this."

"And I tore a hole in my pants at school yesterday!"

"See what I mean?" I say to the others. "It's not DeSean. The lucky person is a boy at our school. His name is Patrick Bell."

That gets their attention again. I can see Jeffrey's mouth open and shut. I know the gears must be turning. He and DeSean both went to those basketball games. They watched the game-winning shots that Patrick made.

"How do you know?" Jeffrey asks. "That he's been lucky? Isn't everyone lucky sometimes?"

"Let's see." I start counting the list off on my fingers. "He had two full-court shots to win games. He won a shoe lottery for the rarest pair of sneakers in existence. He saved a kid from drowning two days ago. In the last

245

basketball game, he didn't miss a single shot and set the school record for points . . . even though the rest of the team *didn't even score*. Does that sound like a normal amount of luck to you?"

Skyler jumps in. "And I wrote down the date that I first made him a cookie. Before that, nothing was going right for him. After he started eating those cookies, it all changed. I wrote about it in my journal."

"That's also when the bad luck started," I say, hoping to keep their attention. "The curse started spreading. Patrick Bell's first victims were Patrick Adams and Patrick Connors. One had a robot explode during a competition. The other broke his wrist *and* was in a car accident. We think they were first because they have the same name and go to the same school. But the curse didn't stop there. . . ."

"I kept giving him cookies," Skyler says. "Which means his luck kept growing . . ."

"According to Mary's calculations," I say, "this curse will be big enough to take down the entire eighth grade. Every single one of us, except for Patrick Bell, will be unlucky."

Avery makes an a-ha noise. "I was wondering why you were the only ones who raised your hands."

"The spell spreads based on proximity," I reply. "People who know *all three* of the Patricks. Their classmates. Us."

Jeffrey raises his hand again. "But how long will the curse last? I had that balloon accident the other day. And the dog chased me on the way here . . . so . . . how many more bad luck days do we have to get through? It can't be that bad . . ."

Skyler and I exchange a glance.

"Forever," I answer. "It will last for the rest of your life. We already confronted Patrick. He had the chance to help us end all of this, but he didn't care about what happened to the rest of the eighth grade. Which means it's up to us. We have to stop him before it's too late."

Before the doomsday officially happens, I think. *Before we get past the point of no return.*

There's silence as everyone considers my words. Jeffrey looks thoughtful. DeSean is shaking his head. Sophie—who is always so focused on taking action—cracks her knuckles.

"Got it. So, what's the plan?"

CHAPTER TWENTY-TWO

The Plan

You're on the yearbook staff, DeSean. Can you confirm the schedule?"

He nods. "I'll look into it. I definitely know the Most Valuable Player ceremony happens about an hour into the dance."

"And you think he'll be the MVP?"

Jeffrey nods. "Absolutely. He's a legend . . . I mean . . . now we know why he's a legend. But everyone else in the school thinks he's the next Steph Curry. Which . . . he probably will be . . . if we fail. Except we won't because we've got a plan!"

"He'll definitely be MVP," DeSean agrees. "And the ceremony has a very specific order. Each MVP walks up onstage with the other MVP from their sport. Boys' basketball is with girls' basketball. Boys' soccer is with girls' soccer. If they don't have a matching sport, then they're at the back of the line and they walk up by themselves. Which means Patrick will be walking with . . ."

"Destiny Jones," Tatyana supplies. "I've watched a few of their games. She's averaging like eighteen points and ten rebounds a game. She'll be the one walking with him."

"Hmm," I say. "Any chance we can get her to help us?"

"Help us do what, though?" Jeffrey asks. "Have we decided how to embarrass him?"

Everyone is on board with the plan. I'm surprised that we didn't have to convince anyone. After hearing what Patrick Bell said the other day in the bakery, no one has any problem embarrassing him in front of the entire school. Besides, it all lines up. Patrick Bell's good luck, and the bad luck that's spreading as a result. Only Tatyana is still skeptical, but I can tell she really likes problem-solving. The deeper we've gotten into the planning, the more excited she sounds.

"I think a trip, onstage, is the way to go," Mary answers. "I've been running through the probabilities of everything. A faceplant is the most likely to work. Keep in mind, though, that his luck will be protecting him the whole time. This isn't going to be easy. But if we can get him to trip and fall in front of the entire school? That should be embarrassing enough to break through."

"Okay," I say. "How do we make that happen . . ."

We talk through ideas. DeSean promises to get us the *exact* order of the sports MVPs who will be called up onstage. Avery mentions a trapdoor they used to use for school plays. That means we'll have access underneath where Patrick will be walking. The only person who might be able to get on the actual stage is DeSean, who can volunteer to take the pictures for the yearbook. But I also don't want him to get caught tripping Patrick in front of the whole school. Something like that could get him in serious trouble. A rope or a wire would probably be too obvious. Besides, no one has a good idea for how to install something like that without tripping the wrong person first. I imagine all the players will be coming up onstage with just a few seconds between each of them.

"Wait," Jeffrey says. "*Agent Zero: Curse of Time!*"

I roll my eyes. "I told you, it's not like that . . ."

"No! In that movie there's this scene where they're trying to steal something from the museum. Remember, DeSean? The golden chicken scene?"

After a second, DeSean grins. "And they use the stairs!"

They're both nodding at each other like this is the most genius thing that anyone has ever come up with. "I'm afraid to ask," I say. "But how does this relate to what we're talking about?"

"How do we trip him without anyone seeing us?" Jeffrey asks. "We go *under* the stairs. If there's a trapdoor on the stage, there should be an entire room down there, right?"

Avery nods. "Yes. It's kind of like a weird supply room."

"Then we'll be able to access the staircase from below. We can unscrew the bolts from one of the steps. I know how to do it. I helped my dad redo our entire back porch last summer. So, when the other athletes walk across, we hold the board steady. But when Patrick's name gets called, we pull it away at the very last second. He misses a step, falls on his face, and the spell breaks. Game over!"

My eyes dart over to Mary. She's nodding along.

"It might work," she admits. "His good luck will make everything else really hard. You almost have to take him completely by surprise, you know? Something fast enough that the good luck can't react. If you time the movement just right, it could definitely work."

I nod. "How do we get under that stage?"

Avery walks through everything she can remember from her time in theater. Slowly an actual plan begins to form. I already know it won't be easy. There are a lot of things that could go wrong. But if we pull this off, everything goes back to normal. I can picture Patrick Adams at his next robotics competition, taking home a blue ribbon. Patrick Connors visiting the skate park, having fun and not worrying about breaking yet another bone.

Pull this off, and we save the entire eighth grade.

"Now that we have a plan," I say, "it's time for my big request. I know that most of us were planning to go to the dance already, but I think all of us have to go. Not just the eighth graders."

Tatyana raises an eyebrow. "Dances aren't my thing."

"Same," Avery says. "They just smell weird. Like gym class mixed with cologne."

"They're not my thing either," Mary replies. "But Celia's right. We all need to be there. Patrick's luck is going to do everything it can to stop this from working. Celia, Jeffrey, DeSean, Sophie, and Skyler are all cursed. Each of them is *unlucky.* The rest of us are like special chaperones. We're not cursed, which means we can avoid some of the traps they'll fall into that would make the plan go wrong. If we're not there, it's possible they'll be too unlucky to pull any of this off."

Tatyana sighs. "Fine."

Avery eventually nods.

"Which brings me to awkward request number two . . . ," I say. "We really need both of the other Patricks to be there. If one of them doesn't show up, the spell might not completely reverse. We need the first two sources of the bad luck to be in the building when it happens."

"I'll ask Patrick Adams," Skyler volunteers quickly. "Wow. That was desperate sounding. It's just that after falling for the jerk, I wouldn't mind spending time with someone nice. Celia showed me his YouTube channel the other day. He seems super cute."

"Great," I say, nodding. "Anyone want to ask Patrick Connors?"

Avery sighs. "I know him from the skate park. I'll ask him."

"And I'll sign up as a chaperone," Mary says. "They always need volunteers. Tatyana, you can be my date."

When Tatyana hears that, her disdain for going to a dance finally breaks. She looks Mary up and down before grinning. "Deal."

"I'm taking Celia!" Jeffrey announces proudly.

"Yeah, we know," DeSean laughs. "You've been talking to us about how you were going to ask her for like three weeks, man."

Sophie throws an arm around DeSean, which immediately cuts off his laughter.

"I'll take you. Which means we're all set. Anything else?"

We're all looking excitedly around the room. I'm pretty sure that everyone understands what's at stake. The idea that five of us could be cursed permanently is a big deal. The easel is full of scribbled plans and poorly drawn maps of the stage. We need to work out all the details, but this is a great start. I'm about to call it a night when a throat clears up on the landing above us.

Everyone jumps. I forgot that Mom was home, and I have no idea how long she's been standing there. She leans against the banister, an eyebrow raised.

"So . . . what's all this?" she asks.

"Just making a plan for the dance!" I answer, hoping she'll accept that version of events.

"Oh? That's all? I could have sworn that I heard something about a doomsday, good luck cookies, and breaking some kind of magical spell?"

The room is full of nervous glances. It's that moment

when we're not sure if we've been caught, if we're all about to be in a lot of trouble. But Mom is more accustomed to my weirdness than anyone else. She points a warning finger at the entire group.

"Nothing illegal. No stealing or breaking anything. No lying to any adults. Got it?"

We all answer her at the same time. The thunderous *Yes, ma'am* has Mom smiling to herself. Before she can head back inside her room, though, I call up to her.

"Wait. We need a backup plan. What do you say, Mom? Want to be my backup plan?"

She looks completely surprised. My mom has always avoided magic. It's always been a touchy subject because it's the one world I belong to that she'll never fully understand. She even missed my 4,444th day, choosing to go to work instead. Now, though, she raises a curious eyebrow.

"What did you have in mind?"

The gears are turning in my head. Everyone is waiting to hear my answer. I can't help grinning as I think about the other option for embarrassing Patrick, if the first plan falls through.

"How long can you last on the Peloton?"

She grins back at me. "My longest class was two hours. Why?"

I'm already thinking through spells. Mary's watching me curiously.

"Because water is '*an ideal but temporary conduit for magic.*' Two hours just might be enough. Okay. Here's the backup plan..."

CHAPTER TWENTY-THREE

Under the Stage

The next two days are a furious rush of preparation.

Tatyana and Mary are both confirmed as chaperones for the dance. Avery reports that she's a green light to attend with Patrick Connors. But that's about where our good fortunes end.

DeSean is too late to cover the dance for yearbook. All the spots were already taken, and that limits some of our access. Especially near the stage. He does manage to sneak a picture of the MVP list so that we know the order they'll walk up. The only problem is that the picture of the list throws *another* wrench in our plans: Jeffrey is the MVP for the boys' soccer team.

"Whoa," he says at lunch. "That's so cool."

"But," I counter, "it also means you can't be under the stage to help with the staircase."

"Oh. Right. Do . . . do you want me to not go onstage? I can just accept the award later. You're right, this is the priority. I'll just ignore . . ."

I wave that thought away. "No chance. You deserve it. Unlike Patrick Bell. Besides, they'll just keep calling your name and the delay will interrupt everything. You have to go."

He looks slightly relieved. "But who will be under the stage with you?"

We keep making small alterations to the plan because the bad luck curse keeps throwing curveballs as the clock ticks down. The last task is to actually get under the stage and see if our main plan can even work. Our first attempt to sneak down there happened to line up with auditions for the next school play. There was no way to get to the lower room without being seen by a lot of people. The second attempt was cut off by a fire drill, which had us being escorted outside with the rest of school. On the final day—the day of the dance—Jeffrey and I head there during lunch.

He got a haircut for the dance. It looks really good. A little tighter on the sides, but with that familiar toss of brown hair bouncing on his forehead. He's wearing a button-down, too, because the MVPs all took pictures together earlier. I can't help thinking he looks really handsome as we arrive at the back door to the theater.

And our bad luck streak continues. The room under the stage is occupied. Mr. Simms comes huffing out from below. He's wheeling a stack of folded chairs behind him. I nudge Jeffrey's shoulder. "What do you think? Come back later? Maybe during fifth period?"

"I have a better idea," he says, clearing his throat. "Mr. Simms? Do you need some help putting out chairs for the dance?"

Before I can say anything, Jeffrey is standing next to the janitor, offering our services. Mr. Simms smiles. "Sure. If you two have a second. I had someone coming for detention, but they're absent. Why don't you grab the next stack? Flip those lights on and be careful wheeling them out."

I try not to look too surprised as he walks past us, tugging the first set of chairs behind him. He aims for the side ramp without even a glance back. Just like that, we're in. The door creaks open. Jeffrey flips the first switch and dusty fluorescents flicker on. A ramp leads down into a room that's become a collection of castaway theater props. There are stacks of folded chairs on dollies. Deflated basketballs. An abandoned piano. Even the previous play's scenery is down here gathering dust.

"Over there."

Jeffrey leads me to the far corner. It's a little darker, but sure enough, the ceiling starts to slant down. It's the spot where the stairs join with the front left corner of the stage. Jeffrey ducks down a little and uses his phone as a flashlight. He points it upward.

"See these screws? You need to take out this one and this one. The step should pop right out after that. But you want to hold it steady until Patrick walks across. I'm pretty sure it's going to lift front to back. Like this."

He mimes with his hand. A motion that would have the stair moving toward the stage, vertically into the air. After a few seconds, he reaches into one pocket and takes out a screwdriver. He carefully places it so that it's out of sight from the rest of the room—but easily accessible for when we come back here tonight.

"There's a big enough crack that you can see out. Right here. That way you can time it just before he takes a step. I'm—I'm sorry I can't be down here with you. I really mean it. I don't have to go up onstage—"

For some reason, his words tangle in my mind. A thought pulses louder than anything he's saying. An echo of moments like this one. Not a glimpse at the future, but the inevitable flow of the past. All the times we've almost kissed. I thought I'd see the moment coming from a mile away. I thought maybe it would be somewhere fun, a scene right out of a movie. But as I stand there in the semidark—listening to kind, sweet Jeffrey—it hits me that this is the boy who

Grammy decided to save. She saw something in him.

And I see it too. I like the way he smiles at me. And I like the way he always reaches for my hand when he wants to show me something. I like how kind he is and how he never asks for anyone to praise him for it. I like the way he slings his soccer bag over one shoulder and how much he loves his family. I like all of those things, and so much more.

Thought transforms into action. Before he can explain how the bolts work, I cut him off with a kiss. It's not a perfect, fairy-tale kiss. We almost miss entirely. He's a little tall and a little surprised. Which means I barely reach his bottom lip. I hear a brief gasp of a breath, and then he leans down and kisses me back. I wouldn't have picked the stairs beneath the theater stage, but sometimes you don't get to flawlessly map out the best moments of your life. Sometimes they just happen to you, and they happen in a way that you could have never predicted. I kiss Jeffrey Johnson and realize that sometimes there's magic in not knowing what's coming.

The distant squeak of a cart has us pulling away. I stretch on tiptoes and kiss him one more time on the cheek, just for good measure. "Thanks for always helping me."

And then we're both moving toward one of the chair racks, made awkward by the bright lights overhead. Not to mention the fact that Mr. Simms is strolling back down the ramp.

"Sorry," he says. "Forgot to tell you how to unlock the wheels. It's a little tricky to figure out. Like anything else, it just takes some practice . . ."

Jeffrey catches my eye and we both fight back smiles. Mr. Simms leans down to show us the unlocking mechanism on the massive chair rack. *It takes some practice.* I'm still smirking about that thought. This might be the first time in my life I'm excited about the idea of *practicing* something besides my magic.

The two of us wheel out the next set of chairs. We keep sneaking glances at each other. This moment is too bright for Patrick's curse to cast a shadow over. There's no amount of bad luck in the world that can quiet the steady pounding of my heart. No curse that can steal my smile. I just had my first kiss, and it wasn't at all how I imagined it would be.

It was better.

CHAPTER TWENTY-FOUR

Preparation

I'm floating a little after kissing Jeffrey, but that just means I hit the ground even harder when five p.m. arrives. We have two hours until the dance. Two hours to take a breath, go over the plan, and make sure that Patrick Bell doesn't ruin the lives of every single eighth grader at our school. Our crew agrees to meet back at the house to discuss final details and finish getting ready for the dance.

It's the getting-ready part that somehow has me the most nervous. Mom was working from home today. At some point, she went through my closet and ironed my five best dresses.

Each one is set out on the bed. I know tonight isn't about this. It's not about how I look, or how Jeffrey looks. But I'm also secretly hoping that I get to dance with him after we save the day. That'd be a nice way to celebrate our victory. If we actually manage to pull this off, of course.

I choose a lavender dress with fun sleeves. Partly because I can imagine Jeffrey saying, *Wow, I love that color!* But mostly because I just really like fun sleeves. Grammy always bought me cute bangles at the jewelry market she'd visit. I fish a few out of my bedside table. They always felt a little too fancy to wear to gym class, but this actually feels like the right occasion for them. Most of the dances are casual. You wear what you'd wear to school, maybe with a nice jacket or hat.

This dance is supposed to be slightly fancier. I remember last year some of the eighth-grade girls treated it like a real prom. That has me feeling like I can get away with a few shiny bracelets and some strappy heels. I can look the part without drawing too much attention. I give myself a once-over in the mirror before heading downstairs.

Mom's not downstairs, though. I'm looking around from

room to room, hoping she'll get the last button of my dress for me, when I hear a *clunk* outside. A rattle follows that. I poke my head out the front door and find Mom bent over by the flower beds.

She's patiently watering the hydrangeas on the far right corner of the house. It's like looking at an echo from the past. She's even got on the old straw hat that Grammy used to wear to keep the sun off her face when she would garden. I haven't thought about the flowers since Grammy died. They were her thing. A beloved chore. It didn't occur to me that with her gone, all of them should have died by now too.

As I take in the rows, though, I realize Mom has been tending to them all this time, because they look as healthy as they ever have. She picked up where Grammy left off. She kept this small part of who Grammy was alive, the same way I did with my magic. The image of her on her knees, surrounded by old yard tools, tugs at the corners of my heart. Grammy's death was a surprise to both of us when it happened. We both grieved together. But I also know *why* it happened. I have a part of the story that Mom doesn't. Almost on cue, she looks up and notices me. Her face breaks into the biggest grin.

"Well, look at you," she says. "Just beautiful, Celia."

My voice sputters out. "Will—will you button me up?"

I turn to show her the button I couldn't reach. She smiles again, pushes to her feet, and starts walking across the yard. My heart's hammering in my chest. I want to tell her everything. I don't want there to be a secret between us, but I also don't want her to have a reason to hate magic. I don't want her to blame the thing that I love—and the thing that Grammy loved—for her own mother's death. The same way Avery blamed our magic for her parents' divorce. I'm sweating by the time she reaches me. I watch as she tosses her gloves onto the porch and reaches for the button.

"Mom," I say. "I need to tell you about something."

She starts patiently working the button through the fabric. "Sure, honey."

"So Grammy . . . She died . . ."

My mom circles around to look me in the eye. "Yes. I am aware of that."

"Well, her death wasn't . . . It wasn't exactly . . . I don't know how to explain it. Last year, my first vision wasn't normal at all. It was actually a death vision. I watched Jeffrey Johnson die."

Mom's eyebrows shoot up as high as they can go. "Jeffrey?"

"Yes. First in a car accident. Then he fell off the bleachers at school. And then there was one at a construction site . . . I saved him each time. I stopped his death from happening, again and again. But death wouldn't give up. Jeffrey was supposed to die. It was like I was . . . stopping fate."

I can see Mom's mind working overtime. She is a lawyer, after all. Her mind wants to connect all the dots and see the whole picture. I do my best to give it to her.

"So in the guide book . . . there was this one page that Grammy ripped out like decades ago. And on that page, there was an explanation for the *only* way to actually stop death. It said that . . . that a seer could sacrifice themselves. If they took the place of the victim, death would be satisfied. A life for a life."

Now Mom's eyes go wide. "But Celia . . . You didn't . . ."

"No. I mean, obviously I'm here. I didn't know about the trade. Instead, I just kept saving Jeffrey. Delaying the inevitable. That's why my grades were so bad. Not making excuses, but I had to keep figuring out how to save him each time," I explain. "But then the final vision. It was taken from me. I only saw the very first glimpse of it. And I didn't know why, but Grammy was the one who stole it from me. She saw that I was going to sacrifice myself to save Jeffrey's life. And she wasn't going to let that happen."

A tear slips down Mom's face, and I realize—out of nowhere—that I'm crying too. It's almost like I've been crying about this ever since Grammy died, but no one else could see the tears. I'm just thankful that I didn't try to put on any makeup yet. It would be a mess.

"She died to save me, Mom. She used her magic. I don't . . . I don't understand why it manifested the way it did. I know the doctors said she had a lot of health issues we didn't know about. Blockages in arteries or whatever. I really don't know how long she would have lived if she didn't sacrifice herself. And I didn't want to tell you because it's *my* fault. I didn't want you to get mad at me. I didn't want you to hate my magic, and I just want Grammy to come back—"

Mom cuts me off with the biggest hug. She wraps me up and squeezes so tight that the rest of my words—all of the thoughts that have been haunting me these past few months—merge into a single, choked breath. It makes me feel like I'm three years old again. Like I've got a skinned knee and it felt like the world would end until the moment that I was in my mom's arms. The pain doesn't go away. The hurt is still there. It's just that, for a second, I'm safe.

"Oh, Celia. I'm so sorry that you've been carrying all of this around. That's a lot. Honey, you know you can tell me *anything*. I would never be mad at you for being who you are. I would never be mad at Grammy for that either. I might not have any magic, but I promise you that if your life was on the line, I would make the same choice. I know that . . . I know I don't understand that part of your life very well. And I know one reason for that is that I didn't want to understand it. Not until Grammy passed away. I avoided talking about it. I'm sorry for that."

She pulls away just enough so that she can look me in the eye.

"But I want to understand. I want to be there for you. I promise you that I'm not mad, honey. Honestly, you just gave me one more reason to love and miss Grammy even more. Because this means that she gave me more time with the person I love the most in the whole world."

I feel like there's no way I'll be able to say anything else without bursting into tears again, so I pull her tight for a second hug. We stand there for a while, and it's the most perfect imperfect moment we've ever had.

"Oh. Hi! Sorry. Do you want me to come back?"

Skyler Dawkins is standing on the sidewalk. She's paused a safe distance away because two people crying on their porch together isn't exactly normal. I smile, though, as I remember that Grammy used to say that "normal" was just a setting on the laundry machine. Mom squeezes my hand one more time before turning to our first guest.

"Come on in, Skyler," she says. "Celia and I were just having a little heart-to-heart. In my experience, it helps to get out all the tears *before* taking on a doomsday scenario."

And with that, we head inside.

Mom heads upstairs to get ready for her part. Skyler takes a seat at the kitchen table. I can tell my new friend is nervous, but she looks like a million dollars. She's wearing a dress and a little tiara and I'm pretty sure someone must have cast a spell that transformed her into a princess.

"You look amazing," I say. "Where'd you even find a dress like that?"

She smiles. "It was my mom's. Weird, I know, but she has this whole wardrobe of these old-school dresses. Don't tell her I said this, but they're actually *really* stylish. It's like a whole other era."

I take a seat at the kitchen table, smoothing my dress.

"That's cool. Do you feel ready?"

"For which part?" Skyler says, half laughing. "The part where I'm taking a boy I don't know to our formal? Or the part where I'm trying to save the entire eighth grade?"

"All of it," I reply with a smile. "It gets easier, by the way.

Not all of your magic will lead to a doomsday spell."

"Oh, no worries. I wasn't planning on using it again."

The words are a shock of cold water. Especially after the conversation I just had with my mom. If she can accept magic as normal, it's hard to imagine someone who actually *has* magic deciding to do the opposite. "Wait. What?"

"Yeah. I mean, I know how my magic works now. I pushed this idea of Patrick having a better day into those cookies. Like an invisible ingredient. So now . . . I'll just . . . avoid doing that. It should be pretty easy, I think."

"But this is a gift. You have a power. You can help people, Skyler. Lots of people."

"Like I helped Patrick?" She shakes her head, and those tight curls dance across her shoulders. "First, he never even thanked me. Because he didn't care about *me*. He just cared about all the luck he was getting. And then it led to all this? No thanks. It seems easier to just not use magic. I don't really know what I'm doing. I didn't grow up learning all of this stuff like you did. I'm pretty sure life will be easier without it."

For a second, I'm not sure what to say. It's the exact

opposite of how I feel about magic. I hold up a finger, signaling for her to wait, and cross over to the living room. I've been flipping through the Cleary Family Guide Book the last few days. There are several spells I'll be juggling tonight for the real plan *and* the backup plan. I walk back to Skyler and set the book in front of her.

"Turn to page thirty-three."

Skyler looks skeptical, but she starts flipping through. I watch her eyes get a little wider as she takes in the heading of the section. Her eyes scan down the page. She's reading all about Charmists and the kinds of spells that they can perform. I remember the first time I read the entries that talked about my powers. It's like reading a Wikipedia entry about yourself. Kind of weird and kind of exciting.

"You don't know what you're doing yet, but that book has a lot of answers. And Grammy taught me that you never fully get everything right. No one does. You just get it a little *righter* each time. You don't have to figure all of this out by yourself, Skyler. I'm here. And you can have full access to our family's entire history."

Skyler eyes the book. She uses a finger to trace the different notes scribbled into the margins. I can see the war happening inside her. The idea that one misstep might define this entire world for her. I can't allow that to happen. This side of who we are is meant to be celebrated, not feared. Grammy taught me that much. I lean in the way that Grammy would, and I offer the same mysterious smile she always used to give me.

"You are *literal* magic, Skyler. You will be like sunshine on a rainy day. The reason someone makes the right turn at just the right moment. A seer . . . provides clarity." For once, I don't have to swallow back tears. I'm not sad because the only thing I can feel is pride as I quote Grammy's favorite line. "We inform. We instruct. We encourage. It's our job to bring out the best possible future in this one wonderful life. And now? The two of us get to do that *together*."

Skyler sits up a little straighter. She nods firmly. "Together."

It doesn't take long for the others to arrive. Tatyana's wearing a dark green dress that glitters in the right light.

Mary wears a rose-red jumpsuit that's so cool that I wish I had a matching one. Avery looks kind of like an anime character—a plaid skirt, a pullover sweater, and a bow tie. It's the kind of look that only she could pull off.

The boys are no less impressive. DeSean looks like he's hosting the Oscars. A full tux that I'm pretty sure he had professionally tailored. When I point that out, he nods, and says that he's sponsored by some suit company that wanted a few posts of him with Slug the Pug.

But Jeffrey's arrival is the real showstopper. He waltzes in with a lavender shirt that's the *exact* same color as my dress. Everyone notices and has a good laugh as Jeffrey offers me a side hug. He pulls back to take a good long look at me.

"Whoa. Great minds think alike," he says. "You look amazing. Is this good luck or bad luck? That we're wearing the same color?"

"I'd just call it fate."

Everyone's in a good mood. There's something about getting dressed up, looking our best, that brings out the positive vibes. I stand there for a second, not wanting to interrupt the fun. I don't want to walk through the plan or be serious yet. I don't want there to be a curse at all. I'm standing there, smiling to myself, when Mom sneaks up and wraps an arm around me.

She's in her workout clothes, as planned. "I'll be upstairs when you're ready."

"Thanks for helping, Mom."

"Anything for you, Celia." She makes her motherly appraisal of me. "And what's going on here? Some kind of magic? How'd my little girl with Minnie Mouse sunglasses and wild hair transform into this?"

I smile back at her. "Mom. Stop."

She kisses my forehead before heading upstairs. As I turn to join my friends, I don't notice the upturned edge of the rug. It catches the toe of my shoe and sends me vaulting through the air. There's a frozen moment where I'm airborne. Jeffrey's reaching for me, but he's too far away. DeSean's eyes are wide as saucers. Before I can crash-land on the glass table in the middle of the living room, Mary catches me. The momentum rocks both of us, and the only reason we don't crash to the ground is Avery, who's lunged forward to throw her weight into us too.

I look down to see the strap of my left shoe has completely snapped off. It's like looking at Cinderella's slipper. Except this one doesn't promise that a prince will come searching for me the next day. There's no good fortune written in those broken straps. No, this is a reminder that a curse is working against us tonight. Tripping on the carpet is just the beginning. And we'll need the non-cursed members of our group to pull all of this off. I carefully slide the other shoe off my foot.

"All right. I'm going to get my backup shoes. And then we'll get started."

CHAPTER TWENTY-FIVE

The Dance

Before we leave, I head upstairs.

Mom's sitting on her Peloton. I've spent most of the afternoon stirring a special tea for just the two of us. The spell I chose for our backup plan is pretty complicated. It's also very familiar.

I had to read Grammy's notes about a thousand times. This is a spell I witnessed her pull off with ease. But Grammy had been a seer her entire life. My only hope is in attempting to cast the same spell at a much, much smaller scale. She moved a metaphorical mountain; I'll try to move a molehill.

Even though the spell is a reduced version, I find myself hoping that we won't need it.

Mom and I trade sips from the same tea mug, and then I set a firm hand on her shoulder. The notes suggest forming as many connections as possible. I realize Grammy didn't even use the "key phrase" she suggests in her own notes to pull it off last year. Maybe she thought I'd know she was up to something? Instead, she snuck in the fridge during the middle of the night and stole some of the tea I'd prepared for Jeffrey and me. That was why I didn't have enough. Not because I'd failed to prepare it properly, but because she knew how important it was to create a connection between all three of us. For what would happen later. She really was always two steps ahead.

"Is that it?" Mom asks.

"Keep drinking."

I tighten my grip on her shoulder before saying my chosen key phrase. The guide book notes the importance of enunciation and clarity of intention. Which means I go with the voice I use to make presentations in class and make direct eye contact with Mom.

"Great work. You *deserve* this. Great work. You *deserve* this. Great work. You *deserve* this."

I offer her shoulder one more squeeze, and then I mentally tie off the spell. The magic feels like a loose rope. One end is tied to my right hand, but the other hand is loose and swirling, waiting to be tied to something else. It takes almost all of my mental effort to keep the spell clutched in my mental hand. As I walk back downstairs, I realize Grammy's version of this spell was a thousand times more difficult. She really was an expert at what she did, and I still have so much to learn.

Outside, two cars are waiting. I pile into the back of Mary's old car. Tatyana signals from the car in front of us. My stomach starts to do somersaults as we pull out and head for school. I carefully remove Mary's hourglass from my purse. Most of the sand has piled in the bottom half now. It's a reminder that the moment has arrived. It's now or never. So much could go wrong. So much *will* go wrong. But this really is our final chance to save the day.

I'm wedged in next to Jeffrey, who always looks a little

ridiculous when he's sitting in the middle seat of a car. His legs are way too long. He grins over at me.

"This is going to be epic," he says. "You're going to do great."

He reaches for my hand, and I almost take his before remembering the backup spell. I pull back at the last second, leaving him hanging. "Sorry! Only touch my left hand! Remember?"

"Oh," he says. "Right, right, right . . ."

He reaches out to hold my other hand before realizing that's super awkward. We both grin at each other, though, because if not for the potential doomsday, the only thing I'd want to do as we drive to the dance is hold his hand. There's a lot of stop and go as we head to school. Even though we left early, I can tell we're going to be late. Precious time is slipping through the hourglass.

"We're catching every red light," Mary comments.

"And that bad luck will only get worse," I say. "The closer we get to Patrick Bell."

Even though we're dressed for a dance, there's a shift in

the car now. Everyone looks like they're prepared for battle. The dresses and tuxedos are more like squad uniforms. We pull into the school parking lot. Tatyana's already parked. I see them waiting on the sidewalk. Avery's in conversation with her date for the night, Patrick Connors. He looks pretty excited to be with her. We pile out of the car, and Skyler turns her phone screen so I can see it.

"Patrick Adams is late. His dad's car wouldn't start."

I think through the plan. According to DeSean, we've got about thirty minutes before the MVP ceremony happens. "Do you think Mary should go pick him up?"

Skyler's reading the texts. "No. He's biking here. He didn't want me to think that he'd ditched me."

"And based on our luck, he's probably going to get a flat tire. Okay. Let me know what happens. I'll make sure Mary's ready to jump in the car, just in case. He has to be here for it. . . ."

There are herds of other students, all being drawn with magnetic force to the yawning doors at the back of the school. Most of the girls are wearing sundresses. A few have gone all out with prom dresses that make them look five years older. Our group follows them inside, and I can't help thinking that we're like a heist crew, pretending to blend in with everyone when we're really on a secret mission. A pair of sixth-grade teachers flank the entrance.

"Don't forget to vote for class king! If you're an eighth grader who *hasn't* voted, you can still vote! We've got forms . . ."

I grab one of the flyers. Jeffrey shoots me a look before snagging one for himself.

"Maybe we can vote for Patrick," I say. "Just in case. It might give us a second chance at having him walk up on the stage. . . ."

Tatyana and Mary head to the chaperone table to sign in. A few steps inside the massive room have me feeling like we've arrived in a different world. I look around and realize that—ironically—the theme of the dance is the *future*. Not the kind of future I usually see, but some kind of distant future. At least I think that's the theme?

There are sleek-looking papier-mâché objects hanging

from the ceiling. Every streamer is black or silver. The whole room shines and glints and reflects. On the far wall, the design team hung hundreds of mirrors. Some are even the fun house–styled mirrors that throw absurd versions of the beholder back at them. Music is playing and other students are dancing near the stage.

"There's Patrick Bell," Jeffrey whispers. "Stage right."

I frown, searching. "Where?"

"Stage right is to the left."

"Well, that's just ridiculous . . ."

I finally spot Patrick. He's in the middle of dancing with Kennedy Keepman. No surprise there. She's probably the most popular girl in the eighth-grade class. Who else would the luckiest guy in the world go to the dance with? Kennedy's actually really nice. I had a class with her in sixth grade— and she was always so bubbly. She single-handedly started the trend of white, face-framing highlights at our school last year. And now she gets swept off her feet into Patrick Bell's good luck? She deserves better than that. I watch them spin, and I realize that most of the other students on the dance floor have formed a semicircle around the two of them. Kennedy dips and Patrick shimmies. Everyone else orbits around like the two of them are creating their own gravitational pull.

Skyler interrupts. "Patrick Adams is almost here."

I nod back. "Perfect. Make sure he's inside before the MVP ceremony, okay? If anything goes wrong, get Mary."

She nods a confirmation. I turn to Jeffrey. He naturally reaches for my hand, and I have to pull it away again. "Jeffrey! My hand. Remember? You can't touch it . . ."

The magic is still pooled there. Jeffrey smiles. "Sorry! It's like I reach for your hand every time I get nervous. I don't know why."

I smile back at him. "Okay. Phase one. Sophie and I have to get beneath the stage. Come on, we need to—"

"Oh hey, Celia!" It's one of the Kapowski sisters. "Can you take our picture real quick?"

I stare back at her. "I, uh, well . . ."

Jeffrey sweeps in. "I've got you. I'm an expert photographer."

Their group of friends starts lining up. He turns to me. "Go," he whispers. "I've got this."

I hate to leave his side, but we both knew this wouldn't be a normal dance. At least not until we deal with Patrick Bell. I walk by Avery, who's sipping a drink, deep in conversation with Patrick Connors. She winks as I pass. Mary is near the entrance as planned, ready to respond to any emergencies.

Tatyana is posted up by the door we picked out during our planning, a chaperone tag hanging from the lanyard around her neck. She gives me a "green light" thumbs-up. I signal to Sophie. She and DeSean break away from the table they're standing at and start following me.

As we walk, I can feel the slightest *tug* of magic. Patrick's good luck is working overtime tonight. It forces my eyes back to him on the dance floor. There's almost an audible whisper in my mind. *Like him. Think he's cool because he* is *cool.* I have to shake my head to get rid of those thoughts.

"Focus, Celia."

Before we make it halfway across the room, though, Mrs. Schubert appears.

"Hey, DeSean! Do you mind coming with me for a second? We need an extra hand to do some videography work of Principal Locklear's dance-off. You have the best sense of angles."

DeSean stumbles to a halt. "Uhh . . . I was just . . . about to dance . . ."

"Oh! No problem. It will be just a couple of minutes. I promise."

He glances at me and I shrug, because what's he going to do? Say no to a teacher? It's another dose of bad luck. He promises to be right back, but I know we don't have time to wait. The MVPs will be announced in less than twenty minutes. We need to get in position as soon as possible. DeSean was going to be a part of the distraction crew for helping us get beneath the stage unnoticed. Now we will have to improvise.

Tatyana waits impatiently for us by the door that leads backstage.

"What was that all about?"

"He's helping with something for yearbook," I reply. "Let's keep moving."

I can feel that magnetic pulse of Patrick's magic again, but I push the feeling away. Tatyana opens the door, and she, Sophie, and I head into the backstage area. It seems mostly empty. I can see the remnants of auditions. Abandoned wigs and dresses and random props. We move quietly past that area, circling around to the back of the stage. My map of the place wasn't perfect, but it leads us to the same spot that Jeffrey and I visited the other day. The only problem is that there's someone waiting there already.

A teacher. I can't believe our bad luck. Why would they post a teacher here? Is it really necessary to guard the backstage area? But as we stand there, peeking around the corner, I realize that he's looking at his phone. He's not actually *guarding* the place or anything. He probably just snuck back here to have a few minutes by himself. Sophie's voice is barely a whisper in my ear.

"What do we do?"

"Make something up? Maybe we can tell him . . . I don't know. Something broke? Or a teacher needs him back in the main room?"

"No," Tatyana hisses back. "Your mom said no lying. Besides, what happens when he goes over to that teacher and realizes they never asked for him? He'll get suspicious. He'll come back here looking for all of us. That's the last thing you want."

"Okay. Then what?"

Tatyana shrugs. "Wait for him to leave?"

"With our luck?" I reply. "He'll be here all night if we're counting on that."

"Fine," Tatyana says. "Wait here. Girl, if I get in trouble . . ."

She slips out of her heels, cracks her neck, and starts sprinting. Most of my time spent with Tatyana has been inside her car. Those moments were always breathless. She drives fast, and her speed doesn't change much now that she's on foot. She races past the spot where the teacher is standing. He looks up from the glow of his phone, looks back down, and then does a double take.

"Hey! Where are you going? Wait!"

And then he's gone, jogging after her, clearly confused why a girl just went sprinting down the hallway into some other section of the school. Sophie and I exchange a glance.

"Well. It's now or never."

We race to the door. A glance down the hallway shows the teacher vanishing around another corner, calling again for Tatyana to stop. I hope she knows where she's going and doesn't get into any trouble. Sophie reaches for the door handle.

"You've got to be kidding me," she says. "It's locked!"

I didn't even think about the fact that it might be locked. It wasn't when we came the other day, but that's because Mr. Simms was down there. I try the handle before eyeing the door frame. I used to know how to use a credit card to open a door, but that trick won't work on this particular door because it's a dead bolt. I'm still trying to figure out what to do when someone turns the corner.

"Need these?"

It's Mary. She dangles a set of keys out. I have no idea where she got them—or how she knew we'd need them. But then I remember she's a seer, a master of probabilities. She grins at me as she sorts through the keys and picks out a golden one with tight ridges.

"My senses tell me that this one has the highest *probability* of working. Hurry up."

"You're a lifesaver, Mary."

She heads back in the direction she came as Sophie and I close the door behind us. I reach for the lights, but Sophie snatches my arm at the last second. "No lights, remember? Someone will see the glow from the wings if we turn them on."

"Right," I say. "Thanks."

We use the light of her phone to maneuver around random objects. The underside of the stairs is waiting for us. I reach into the nook where Jeffrey left the screwdriver, half expecting it to be gone, but it's there. Our first lucky turn.

"Hold your light right here. I think this step will be the easiest one for us to work with. . . ."

Sophie holds up her phone, and I patiently find the two screws that Jeffrey mentioned. The first one unwinds easily. *Righty-tighty, lefty-loosey,* I think. It turns and turns until it pops out. I hand the little bolt to Sophie before starting on the next bolt. *One rotation, two rotations . . .*

Snap.

"What on earth . . ."

Sophie holds her phone a little higher, and we both let out groans. The screwdriver actually *broke*. The head snapped in half. I pick up the toothed end and try to work the bolt with it, but without the handle to grip, it's almost impossible to turn the thing. Besides, it looks like I stripped the bolt with that last attempt.

"Let me try," Sophie says.

We exchange tools. I hold her phone as she tries to keep rotating the screw with her hand. She even uses a sleeve, trying to get more traction. Nothing. I move forward and give the step a testing shove, but with that bolt still secured, it doesn't even budge. There's no way for us to trip Patrick if we can't get the second one out.

"Search the room. Maybe there's something else in here we can use?"

Music booms overhead. We can hear snatches of people laughing or cheering. I know the clock is ticking. We probably have five minutes at most before our first chance to embarrass Patrick Bell. And there's no guarantee we'll get a second chance. Sophie tests out a few other objects. We're both getting desperate, even searching the lining of old costumes. My heart races when a loud thump sounds by the entrance. We both go still for a second, but the door doesn't open.

"Find anything?" I ask.

Sophie's on her hands and knees in one corner. "No, nothing . . . wait . . . wait . . ."

She rushes across the room, banging her knee on an abandoned dresser in the process. I squint a little as she holds up what she's found. We both grin at each other like fools. There's no way.

"A lucky freaking penny," Sophie says. "Maybe some kinds of luck are too old to be beaten by Patrick's spell. . . ."

It takes a few more turns, but the bolt gives way. The step is loose. We carefully test out the motion, trying not to draw attention. Sure enough, the entire board wiggles free. It's just like Jeffrey said. It will move *up* and *back* toward the stage. When we move it, there'll be a large enough gap that Patrick will step straight down. A guaranteed fall. Sophie settles the step back into the right position. I make sure that we can hold the board steady for now without anyone noticing it's loose.

A second later, we hear the music stop overhead. Principal Locklear is onstage. His voice echoes out. "All right, everyone. Gather around. It's time to announce this year's most valuable players in every sport. And yes, that *does* include our amazing chess team!"

There's a cheer. The sound of people gathering. I lock eyes with Sophie in the dark.

"It's time."

". . . if all the athletes who were notified earlier this week could come up. Yes, line up over here, thank you. All right . . . First up we have Everett Willis . . ."

I try to steady my breathing. Timing is *everything*. More names are called. One by one, the MVPs walk up the stairs above us. I hear Jeffrey's name. As he walks, he double taps the exact step that we're waiting under. I imagine him smiling, knowing that I'm down here in the dark.

"And of course, Patrick Bell for the basketball team! What a run they've had lately. He's joined by Destiny Jones from the girls' squad. Destiny is also having a record year! Come on up . . ."

I squint a little. Sophie's shoulder is pressed to mine. This is it. The moment we planned for is here. She sets her hands on one half of the step. I set mine on the other half. We hear the loudest cheers yet from the audience. And then I spot a flash of Patrick's lottery-ticket shoes through the cracks. He's walking up before Destiny does. I whisper to Sophie, and we wait for the last possible second. Timing is everything. Mary said we needed to take the good luck by surprise.

The first step creaks. Another one.

"Now."

We push the step up and it's *flawless* timing. The missing board gives us a narrow view up. Patrick Bell's eyes are fixed on the crowd. He doesn't see us at all. He doesn't hear the groan of wood. There's too much happening to notice the slightest shift of the ground beneath his feet.

I watch as his right foot rises, as it prepares to set down in empty air. He will fall forward. It will be a total faceplant in front of the whole school, and the spell will *finally* break.

But the magic around him flexes in the air.

It all happens so fast. The step we're holding is vertical. Just a narrow strip of wood that should be completely unstable. Patrick's foot course-corrects, though. It sets down *perfectly* on that slender section of wood. Somehow he keeps walking up the stairs without missing a beat.

Instead of him, it's Destiny Jones who falls. We watch her foot plunge down toward us. Her arms pinwheel. I'm staring in shock, horrified that we embarrassed the wrong person. But of course, Patrick turns at the very last second. He catches her just before she can hit the ground.

There's an absolutely *massive* cheer from the crowd. The two of them take the stage, and people are going wild in the audience. Patrick stops to take a quick bow. Sophie and I stare at each other, and then we're scrambling to get the step back into place. We're both standing down in the dark, our chests heaving. She says the words that I'm thinking. Impossible words.

"The good luck didn't just save him. It made him look like the hero. Again!"

I grit my teeth. "Time for the backup plan . . ."

CHAPTER TWENTY-SIX

Backup Plan

W hat happened?" DeSean asks. "It looked like you moved the step a second too late!"

Our crew has gathered at the back of the auditorium. Everyone except for Avery, who's out on the dance floor with Patrick Connors for a semi-awkward-looking slow dance.

"We *weren't* a second late," Sophie answers. "It worked. It *should* have worked. Patrick performed some kind of tightrope-walking miracle without even looking. What he just did . . . It was impossible."

"There's still the backup plan," I say, nodding at Mary.

"We just have to make sure that Patrick goes onstage again. What are the odds, Mary? Of him winning formal king?"

Mary looks like she's seeing math equations float through the air.

"Right now, it's a coin flip. But the odds of you using your magic on him before the doomsday event happens are way lower. Still, there aren't any other options. This is our last shot."

"First step is to make sure he wins," I announce. "Let's go vote for Patrick Bell."

At the back of the room, there's a stretching table full of different attractions. Collages of the different school clubs and their activities. A sign-up for the end-of-year field trip. On the far right side, I spot the voting booth with a pair of crowns decorating the top. An entire fleet of teachers are standing behind the connected tables, watching the dance with a mixture of amusement and boredom. We head that way.

Mary and Tatyana are forced to circle the room, trying to keep up appearances as good chaperones. I'm half expecting a teacher to give us a hard time at the voting booth. Maybe they'll interrogate us on whether or not we've already voted. But no one even looks our way. I realize that this is Patrick Bell's good luck at work. Of course they're not going to ask us about that. The world *wants* him to win.

I scribble his name on a slip of paper before shoving it in the ballot box. DeSean, Sophie, and Jeffrey all follow suit. Skyler's still out in the middle of the dance floor with Patrick Adams. He looks—surprisingly—like he's having the time of his life. I smile at the expression on his face.

That little glimpse fuels my determination. He won't get many moments like this if we don't stop Patrick Bell. We need to execute the backup plan. Skyler sees me watching them and whispers something to her Patrick. He heads over to get both of them sodas as Skyler walks our way.

"What happened?"

"The first plan didn't work. Round two. Go vote for Patrick Bell."

Skyler heads straight for the voting booth. I spot Principal Locklear off to the right side of the stage. He's talking with a few of the other teachers. He's the one who will announce the king and queen. Maybe we can distract him? Buy ourselves more time somehow?

I'm about to suggest something when it happens. Patrick Adams is returning with two cups of soda. He trips, though, and I watch as a slow-motion stream of Coke comes pouring through the air, aimed directly at me. I'm bracing myself for the inevitable soaking when someone grabs my hand and pulls me out of the way. Jeffrey's there. He tugs me clear of the splash, keeping me steady on my feet. Patrick Adams is all apologies, but Jeffrey and I both make the same realization at the same time.

"Oh no . . ."

He grabbed my *right* hand. The spell waiting there thunders forward. A dash of sweat appears on Jeffrey's forehead as he looks at our clasped hands. I barely manage to sever the connection before the entire spell releases. I feel all of that magic stutter to a halt. Jeffrey isn't hit by the full impact of the spell, but I can tell the magic is no longer pooled in my palm. The spell has slipped through my literal and metaphorical fingers. It's gone.

"No, no, no! Celia. I'm so sorry . . . I wasn't thinking . . ."

Skyler pulls an apologetic Patrick Adams away, promising it's not a big deal. But that is exactly what it is: a big deal. A very big deal. Mary appears at my side.

"What just happened? Our probability of succeeding just dropped a ton. . . ."

"The backup spell," I say. "Jeffrey accidentally grabbed my hand. I need to get back home and reestablish the spell. Now."

"Come on," Mary calls back. "I'll drive."

"No, we need to move *fast*. We need Tatyana."

Mary nods. She flags the other girl down. Jeffrey's a mess. He keeps blaming himself.

"You were just trying to help. It's okay. I promise, it's okay. I just need to go home and redo the spell. We'll be back as soon as we can. . . ."

"What can we do?" Jeffrey asks. "While you're gone?"

Skyler has reappeared. Sophie and DeSean are waiting too.

"I'm pretty sure Patrick will be the king," I say. "It's a gut feeling. The luck is swaying everything in his favor. But we can't let him get back onstage until I get back. Do whatever you can to delay the announcement. Anything you can think of to buy us time!"

I've never liked giving up control of anything, but right now, I have no choice. This crew of friends is all I have. Besides my magic. And that gives me an idea.

"Skyler. Can you use some magic? Maybe a few good luck charms? One for each person?"

She shakes her head. "But . . . I used cookies last time . . . I don't know . . ."

My eyes dart to the snack table where Patrick Adams just got their drinks. Sure enough, there are several rows of packaged cookies. "Over there. It's not the same as baking them, but I'm sure you can channel some of your magic into those."

"But . . . but what if . . . what if I make everything worse?"

I set both of my hands on her shoulders. "I promise. You've got this. Take your time. Just a little bit of magic in each cookie. I believe in you."

She nods. "Okay. Right. I can do this. Everyone. Come with me."

Tatyana arrives. "What's up?"

"I need to get home. Fast."

She grins. "Your wish is my command."

"I'm coming too," Mary says. "You might need my probability magic."

And without another word, the crew breaks like we were in a football huddle. The three of us head for the back of the gym. I glance over my shoulder once—for the briefest moment—and the world of magic layers over our world. It's like last year at the water park, when I could briefly see death's strings tied around Jeffrey. But this time, there's a golden light at the very center of the dance floor. I know it's Patrick. He's so bright and blinding that it's like trying to look directly at the sun.

Everyone else in the room looks like a shadow in comparison. Their expressions and faces are blurred. Almost like there's smoke circling the air around them. A curse separating them from the joys the world around them has to offer. I spot Jeffrey, standing where I left him. The shadows blur his smile from me, though. He raises his hand and waves, maybe to wish me good luck, but I feel like I'm staring at our future. Some of my favorite people in the world, forever cursed.

I race through the parking lot and climb into the back of Tatyana's car.

"Punch it."

The engine roars.

We're back on the road, and it feels like we're in a race against time itself.

One Final Chance

The way home is easy.

It's almost like retreating *away* from Patrick calms down the amount of bad luck we're facing. Like we're less of a threat to his good luck the farther away we get. Tatyana has the car pulling up to the curb outside my townhome in five minutes flat. I step out from the car a second before we stop, leaping over Grammy's old flower beds and shouldering through the front door.

Upstairs, I can hear the music pumping. A voice is

shouting at Mom, but this time it's coming from inside her room. "This is your Everest! Ascend!"

I shoulder inside. Mom glances at me from across the room. She's covered in sweat, legs still pumping. And she's not alone. Mrs. Monroe from next door is standing beside her.

"You've got this!" Our neighbor pauses to wave at me. "She pulled a muscle back on the fifth mile. She's a true warrior to keep going like this. I don't know how much longer she's got. . . ."

I can tell Mom's been going for a while, just like we planned. She looks exhausted.

"Did it work, Celia? I thought I felt something . . ."

I glance over at Mrs. Monroe, unsure of what I'm allowed to say in front of her. She smiles at me, though. "I was one of your grandmother's longtime customers. She told me your gift runs in the family. No worries. Your secret is safe with me."

My secret—I realize—is safe with a *lot* of people right now. "Right. Okay. The spell released too early. It was an accident. I need to link with you again. Are you sure you can keep going?"

Mom grins back. "Of course. Didn't you hear? I'm climbing Everest."

"We're climbing Everest!" Mrs. Monroe repeats. "You've got this, girl!"

I shake my head. There's no time to laugh, even if it is hilarious. I pick up the tea I made earlier. There's about half a cup left. I learned that from what happened last year. Always leave room for error. A little extra, just in case.

"Here we go again."

The two of us trade sips back and forth as she continues pumping the pedals of the bike. The tea tastes pretty awful, and each sip seems to taste worse than the next. It doesn't help that it's gone cold, either. I set my hand on Mom's shoulder again. I keep my grip firm, feeling for the threads of magic.

"Great work. You *deserve* this. Great work. You *deserve* . . ."

Magic flows between us as I repeat the phrase over and over. I doubt Mom can really feel it, but the same connection pools in my right hand. The one that Jeffrey accidentally touched. The magic is a little weaker this time—and that has me worried—but we don't have time for another plan. I picture the almost-empty hourglass in my purse. We only have so many grains of sand left. We're about to hit the point of no return.

"Thanks, Mom. Thirty more minutes. Okay?"

She keeps pedaling, leaning back over her chair.

"Thirty minutes? I've got this."

"Yeah you do!" Mrs. Monroe roars.

I'm back down the stairs and out the door in no time. Tatyana's not waiting in the car, though. She's on the lawn. Mary is lying flat on her back in the grass.

"I don't know what happened. She just . . . stumbled out of the car. . . . I think she passed out?"

Mary doesn't open her eyes, but her lips form a whisper.

"Put me back in the passenger seat."

She's not moving her limbs at all. Her body is completely limp. Tatyana gets her legs, and I get a grip under her arms. "Mary? What's happening? Do you need to go to the hospital? I don't—"

"Put me back in the passenger seat."

We settle her into the seat. Tatyana works to buckle her in. She's still not moving. And then Mary's eyes snap open. Except they're literally glowing with blue light. Tatyana looks at me, slightly terrified.

"Uhh . . . ," she says. "You see that, right?"

"I do see that. I'm guessing, since you're asking me, that you also see it?"

"Of course I see it. Her eyes are *glowing*."

Mary speaks in a toneless voice. "Now that we're this far from school, the curse is throwing every possible obstacle it can. Follow my directions. Everything I say, understood? Everything . . ."

Tatyana shoots me a look that says *This is wild, what on earth is up with your family?* I just shake my head, though, because this is pretty normal for us. Just with more . . . glowing eyes involved.

"Come on," I say. "Let's go."

I buckle up. Tatyana revs the engine. I can barely hear Mary's voice.

"Forward."

Tatyana pulls out. We pass the park on one side. As she drives, though, ten cars pull out simultaneously from every street. I've never seen anything sequenced so perfectly. The road ahead of us fills up with cars almost instantly. There's beeping and traffic, and it looks like it will take a while to actually pull out of the neighborhood.

"A left here," Mary whispers.

Tatyana whips into a quick turn. Ahead, a woman stumbles out into the crosswalk in the distance, tangled in the leashes of two dogs that are jumping all over each other.

"Take a right. Go all the way to the end of the road . . ."

Tatyana looks like she wants to object, but after glancing back at me in the mirror, she adjusts our course. We veer around the woman and find ourselves on a back road in the neighborhood. Houses slip past as Tatyana starts to pick up speed.

"Use the other side of the road. Watch out for the basketball . . ."

Tatyana swings into the wrong lane, and sure enough, a little boy comes sprinting after his basketball on the right side of the street. If we'd kept going in the correct lane, she would have had to slam on the brakes. She slides safely past instead.

"Take the next left."

Slowly but surely, we make it out onto the main road. At every turn, the forces of the world are swirling in an effort to keep us away from the school. It doesn't seem like we're going to make it, but I also find myself thinking that this is a good sign. Patrick's good luck is *afraid* of us.

There's a fleet of geese crossing the next road. Mary reroutes us. A traffic accident, but Mary swings us into the grocery store parking lot for a shortcut. It happens again and again like that. However, the moment of truth arrives when we get to a construction crew that's cutting off the road I've always taken to school. Mary instructs Tatyana to pull into the adjacent neighborhood. But there's a construction guy with a sign waiting for us here, too.

"Celia. Roll down your window. Wave at him."

I frown at those instructions, but I know better than to question her. Cool air breathes through the open window as we come to a stop. The construction guy leans down.

"Sorry. Can't come this way. Thru traffic . . ." And then we spot each other. I wave at him and he looks at me in disbelief. It's Vincent. From the movie theater. "No way! Soda girl! It's you!"

"Ask him to let us through," Mary whispers.

"Can we get through? We're just driving on the other—"

"Say no more!" he says, waving me on. "Anything for you! Have a good night."

I can't help marveling at the random connection. I didn't know why I was supposed to help Vincent that night. I'd assumed it was just to make his life a little better, but now it's come full circle. I smile at the thought as Mary uses her magic to guide us through a neighborhood that I know she's never set foot in her entire life.

It takes a few more minutes, but we arrive on the back road that leads to the school parking lot. Mary did it. She guided us through every imaginable unlucky twist of fate.

"Let Celia out," she whispers. "A car is going to block us from pulling in . . ."

Tatyana swerves toward the nearest curb. Her chest is

heaving as she looks back to me. I see the glow in Mary's eyes finally fade. Now she really *does* look like she's going to pass out.

"You . . . have . . . one percent chance . . . remember he always . . . dribbles to *his* right . . ."

She sinks down into her seat. Dribbles to his right? That's a basketball term. Is it a hint? Or is she delirious? I shoot a look at Tatyana.

"Go," she says. "I'll take care of her."

I thank Tatyana before opening the door and darting toward the school's entrance. I navigate through the thinning traffic and plunge into the semidark without a second thought. The magic gathered in my right hand is pulsing. A slow dance is almost over. I take a deep breath, searching for my target. Principal Locklear is walking across the stage. He shields his eyes to squint out at all of us.

". . . Mrs. Schubert? Seriously? Can we . . . Okay, folks. It does look like it's going to be just a second. Apologies for the delay. Let's play *one* more song. Just *one*. And then we'll announce the winners . . ."

I don't have to look far to see that things have clearly gotten out of control since I left. Most of our classmates are waiting on the dance floor, eagerly hoping to find out who won queen and king. But most of the teachers have circled around the girls' bathroom area. I see Jeffrey and DeSean pacing nervously nearby. I walk that way.

"Hey," I whisper. "What's happening?"

Jeffrey shakes his head. "Skyler did her best. Her good luck cookies worked but in short bursts. And then we all had sugar crashes. Or bad luck crashes? I don't know. Skyler's over by the drinks, trying to stay hydrated. She almost passed out."

"Got it, but what's with the bathroom? Why are all the teachers over here?"

"We were running out of options," DeSean answers. "Sophie stole the ballot box. She's locked in a bathroom stall, pretending to protest the event."

"Protest? What's she protesting?"

"The celebration of binary genders," DeSean says. "She told them that having one king and one queen is outdated.

They should have just had people vote for whoever. And then had *those* two people decide if they wanted to be a king or a queen. I've heard her say something like that before . . . but she's mainly doing this to buy you time. I don't think she's going to last much longer."

"Sophie is amazing." My eyes roam back to the dance floor. "I need to find Patrick Bell."

"He's untouchable," Jeffrey warns. "I tried to embarrass him while you were gone. I tripped him on the dance floor. It was like reality bent backward to help him. He turned the stumble into a cool dance move. Just like what happened on the stage. I don't think we can beat him. . . ."

"We've got one more chance," I say, trying to summon more confidence than I feel. "DeSean, can you live stream this? If this works, I don't want to risk just embarrassing him in front of this crowd. We need what happens to *really* break through his magic."

He pulls out his phone. "I'll go find the best angle."

"Jeffrey, come with me."

I march across the room to Skyler first. Patrick Adams

is—quite adorably—fanning her as she sits with her eyes half closed. "Hey, Skyler. Any chance you have enough energy for one more..." I consider Patrick and the other students standing within earshot by the snack table. "... boost of confidence?"

Skyler groans a little but sits up. "Bring me a sugar cookie."

I have to slip around the Kapowski sisters and their crew to snag one. Skyler stares at it like someone who has eaten a record-setting amount of cookies, and is now being asked to eat just one more. She sets a hand to her left temple and the other to the cookie. I sense the slightest jolt of her magic. It's not much, but I know that any good luck will help. She slumps as the spell finishes.

"Did I do okay?" she whispers. "I tried my best."

"You were *great*. You're on the volleyball team, right?"

Skyler nods.

"Okay. Think about it this way: you just set the ball for me. Now I'm going to go spike it."

She smirks at that. "You're pretty short to pull off a spike."

"Let's hope Patrick Bell thinks that too."

I shove the entire cookie into my mouth. A few bites, and then I swallow the whole thing. It doesn't take long for the effect to hit. My muscles all tighten at once. I can feel the bright boost of confidence. A firm whisper of a voice in the back of my mind. It tells me to search the dance floor.

Two things happen at once.

First, Sophie reappears. One of the teachers leads her out of the bathroom and has her hand over the ballot box to Principal Locklear. He moves off to one side and has Mrs. Schubert start counting them for the final tally. I know they'll announce the winner in a few minutes.

The second—and more crucial—detail is that Patrick Bell is only human. He might be the luckiest person in the world, but lucky people still have to use the bathroom some-times. I spy him breaking away from Kennedy and heading to the opposite side of the room from where Sophie just appeared. The entire dance floor falters without him. Like they're not sure what their purpose is without the star of the show present. The thought of all of them being manipulated by his good luck has my anger building.

"I'm going in," I say to Jeffrey. "Stay here and keep an eye on me."

I move to intercept Patrick Bell. All of the teachers are distracted by what's happening on the other side of the room. And they're about to announce him as king. It's perfect timing. He's a few steps ahead of me, but I'm gaining on him. I notice that Patrick Bell isn't sweating. Not a blade of hair is out of place. He looks like he just stepped out of a magazine that advertises school dances.

"Hey!"

He spins around, a smile already on his face. It vanishes when he sees that it's me.

"Oh. What do *you* want?"

I'm not here to talk. Now is the time for action. I just have to set my hand on his right shoulder. I need to repeat the same words I said to my mom in the exact same tone. If I can do that, the spell will activate and he'll be embarrassed enough that . . .

. . . but as I reach for his shoulder, the lucky magic activates in full. I thought it was powerful before. I had no idea.

Golden light pours out from him. He looks like a minor deity, backlit by the thunderous glow. My hand freezes in midair. I can't move. The whispered suggestions from before turn into *commands*. I can feel my willpower slip away. It's replaced by thoughts of Patrick.

He's the best. Look at him. He's so cool.

My hand drops back to my side. Patrick waltzes forward with a knowing smile on his face. *A beautiful smile. That really might be the best smile in all of eighth grade. Maybe in the whole world.* I stare up at him dreamily.

"Yes, Patrick? Can . . . can I help you with anything?"

He shakes his head. "How about you just . . . stay right here? For the rest of the night?"

There's literally nothing I could want more in the world.

"Of course. Right here. I'll wait for you."

He smiles again, almost a smirk, and then vanishes into the bathroom. I stand there, dreaming of the moment he'll return. Wow, Patrick Bell talked to me. He asked me to *wait* for him. Does this mean . . . could I really have a chance with him? My mind races ahead, giddy with excitement.

Somewhere in the background, I hear a microphone being tested. Principal Locklear's voice. I don't turn, though, because if I look that way, I might miss Patrick's return. I wait instead.

"All right, we're going to move on with the announcement of our two winners. Out of respect to Sophie's protest, I agree that we should allow each winner to choose their own styling. You can be a queen or a king. Or whatever title you want! It's up to you. Just know that you're all royalty in *my* book! When we call the names . . ."

Another voice. Closer this time. I'm thinking about how *great* Patrick will look in a crown when someone steps into view. It's Jeffrey Johnson. There's some memory—some tug of a thought—but it fades when I see Patrick exit the bathroom behind him. My eyes follow his progress toward the stage. He didn't see me. Not this time. But if I just wait right here, like he told me, he'll come back and maybe we can go get ice cream after the dance. That would be so—

"Celia! What happened?"

Jeffrey's really close. I blink at him. "Sorry. I'm waiting for someone."

He frowns. "Waiting for someone? Who?"

It makes me feel giddy just to say his name. "Uhh. Patrick Bell, of course. He . . . he told me to wait here. I'm sure he'll be back any second now."

Jeffrey stares at me. A distant part of my brain thinks: *Wow, he's kind of cute.* But I know that thought is a betrayal. A betrayal of my *true* love. Patrick is the one I'm waiting to see. Not Jeffrey.

And that's when he kisses me.

There are hoots from other students nearby. I start to pull away, worried about what Patrick will think if he sees us, but Jeffrey kisses me again and something in my mind breaks. It shatters into a thousand pieces. My willpower returns, and I kiss him back. I remember *he* is the one I like. He's the person who makes my heart beat faster. I was just . . .

". . . hoodwinked." I look up at Jeffrey. "You saved me. And now, I can save us."

There's a small circle of students watching our interaction, giggling to themselves. I give Jeffrey a quick kiss and push away. Then I'm running. Up onstage, Principal Locklear is announcing the voting results. "Our first winner is none other than Kennedy Keepman. Kennedy, why don't you come over to the side stage and await your partner in crime. . . ."

I spy Kennedy navigating through the crowd. I can also see Patrick Bell waiting off to one side. There's a smirk on his face because he *knows* that he's going to win. Unfortunately, the crowd is sprawling. There are students everywhere. Everyone is crowding forward to see who the winner will be. Gaps keep closing. I'm not going to make it in time.

"I've got you." Avery is there. She links an arm through mine. "I navigate the high school hallways. Hulking seniors and open lockers and people bumping shoulders. This is *nothing.*"

She guides me through. We're moving fast now. I can tell that there's no way I'd have made it without her. Every time a gap in the crowd closes, Avery ducks us through another one. She's smooth—and uncursed—and we make it to the front of the crowd right as Locklear's voice rings out.

"Our second winner is *the* Patrick Bell! If you'd join Kennedy on the side stage, and both of you can make your way up. Yes! Right up this way . . ."

There's a partition to the right of the stairs that's several feet taller than me. I know they used it earlier to hide the MVPs before announcing their names. It's clear they wanted anyone going onstage to walk all the way around, to the far right, before coming up the steps. Patrick circles that way, and I know my only chance is to cut him off. There's a small gap between the partition and the staircase that was clearly not intended for anyone to try to get through. I aim for it. Avery lets me go. I'm almost jogging. I see Principal Locklear frown as I climb around the wrong side of the barrier. Kennedy is right there, seconds away from taking her first step up the waiting stairs.

She looks surprised to see me. "Oh. Hi . . . Are you . . . with yearbook?"

I don't bother answering. I slide around her without a word. The move leaves me face-to-face with Patrick Bell. He looks up in surprise. I can tell he thought that he'd already dealt with me. The two of us are cut off from the rest of the school by the partition. It's just me and him and the magic swirling around both of us.

"Can you move? They just called my name. . . ."

I take up a defensive stance, though. He's not getting past me that easily. Not this time. Patrick's eyes narrow. Mary's advice echoes at the last second. *He always dribbles to his right.* She watched his basketball videos with me. It was half prophecy and half research. When Patrick fakes to his left and darts the other way, I know what he's going to do. My hand lands on his shoulder.

"Great job," I say, repeating the key phrase. "You *deserve* this."

And this time, it's *my* magic that thunders forward. His good luck shoves back. I can feel the weight of both of them warring briefly in the air above us. For a second, I think it's not going to work. I feel sweat break out on my forehead. He's winning. But I am the granddaughter of a seer, who was a granddaughter of seers. This runs in my veins, and I am not about to be bossed around by a boy who had one too many cookies.

I shove the spell forward until it breaks through his barrier. And nothing happens. Or at least, it doesn't *seem* like anything happens. Patrick Bell looks at me with a weird expression. His good luck is still there, hanging thick in the air around us. He raises a confused eyebrow.

"Uhh . . . thanks, I guess . . ."

And then he's moving past me. He runs up the stairs, clearly eager to get away. I turn to watch with complete satisfaction. He has no idea what my spell just did. There's an answering roar from the crowd as Patrick Bell joins Kennedy onstage. It only takes a few seconds, though, for the cheers to transform into laughter. That laughter booms and echoes. Someone shouts.

"Sweat much, bro?!"

I watch as my spell does its work. Grammy taught me this one last year by accident. I always wondered how she summoned Jeffrey and me back to her bedroom that day, the day she saved him from drowning. I distinctly remembered being *in* the water *in* her bedroom. Months later, I read about teleportation and found out it's almost impossible. It took a while to realize she didn't teleport *us*. She summoned the water, and we just happened to be in that water, which is an ideal conduit for magic.

I just did the same thing on a smaller scale. The connection ran from Mom, through me, to Patrick. All it took was a slight tweak. Instead of water, I summoned sweat. That's why the entire school is laughing right now. Patrick Bell is *covered* in sweat. An hour's worth of sweat, in fact. It's running down his forehead. There are stains under both arms, running up and down his pants. It's embarrassing enough to sweat after gym class at school. But this amount of sweat?

Even his good luck charm can't make this look cool.

Everyone is laughing. I know DeSean is feeding the video out. None of them see what happens next, but I do. The golden light surrounding Patrick *shatters*. All of that good luck is flung back into the room. It flashes bright in the air, curling down and settling back on the shoulders of every eighth grader who had their luck stolen from them already.

I look back in time to see it hit Patrick Adams. He sits up a little bit straighter next to Skyler. He has no idea what happened. It's just a sense that something is *right* again. Patrick Connors reacts the same way. Avery is standing beside him. I see him grin to himself because it probably feels like a gloomy cloud just lifted from over his head.

And it has.

Principal Locklear escorts Patrick Bell off the stage. He hushes the crowd, but I know that we did it. The doomsday scenario is over. The good luck spell has been reversed. It won't keep growing out of control. Everyone is back to normal. My eyes search the room for my crew. The others are all gathering around Skyler. Jeffrey waves for me to come join them. I laugh and start walking across the room.

Finally it feels like we have something to celebrate.

Slow Dance

There's finally time to dance.

It's a slow song—something by John Legend—that has us carving out a corner for ourselves. Jeffrey's hands settle on my waist. I set mine on his shoulders. We turn around the room in a slow circle, and it finally feels like everything is the way it should be. It's the first time in weeks that I've been able to just focus on the boy standing in front of me. Nothing else in the room matters, at least for one song.

"So . . . where'd you learn your Fairy-Tale Kissing skills?"

He shrugs. "I've read a few books on the subject."

"Sophie will be annoyed if she finds out your kiss is what broke the spell on me."

"It's like you said, though," Jeffrey replies. "I saved you so that you could save all of us. You and Skyler are the *real* heroes."

As we circle, I spot Mary over Jeffrey's shoulder. She and Tatyana look like a pair of wallflowers. She waves and Tatyana makes a kissing face. I roll my eyes at both of them. Skyler's been talking with Patrick Adams over at the concession tables for the last thirty minutes. I'm pretty sure he's on the verge of setting a record for his longest conversation in history. Avery and Patrick Connors are sitting at the same table as them. She's way too cool to be at a middle school dance, but right now she's patiently drawing art on his cast like she wouldn't want to be anywhere else in the world.

The *other* Patrick never made another appearance after Locklear took him backstage. I almost feel bad about what we had to do to him. I mean, I transported my mom's sweat onto his clothes in front of the entire school. Not a great look for anyone. I'd feel worse if he hadn't been totally fine with cursing the entire eighth-grade class. I find myself looking around at all the other students, feeling proud of what we accomplished tonight, when Jeffrey steps on my right toe.

"Ouch!"

"Oh no . . . wow. I'm so sorry, Celia. My footwork's normally a strength."

He starts to pull away, but I didn't go toe-to-toe with a doomsday tonight just so I could stop dancing halfway through our first song. I pull him back toward me and smile.

"I know you have good footwork," I say. "I watched all your games. You're very good at . . . center backing."

"Defense," he says, grinning. "We just call it defense. And speaking of defense . . . you were basically the center back tonight."

"I feel like this is a metaphor. Mrs. Dailey would be proud."

The two of us keep turning around. The song ends, but another slow dance follows it. I silently thank the DJ for keeping me in Jeffrey's arms for a few more minutes.

"It's a good metaphor," he says. "The center back has to give clear directions. You did that. You made a plan. You talked us through everything. And a center back can't panic. They have to stay calm so the rest of the defense stays calm. No matter what happens. There were like ten times tonight where you could have totally panicked. But you didn't."

I can't help blushing. I'm still not used to having a boy I like say such nice things about me. It's one thing when Grammy or Mom talks like this. I always kind of felt like they *had* to say those things because we're family. Hearing it from Jeffrey is different somehow.

"And a center back is the last line of defense. We have to make that one crucial tackle to stop the other team from having a free shot. The rest of our school doesn't know it, but you made the tackle tonight. The one that saved all of us. You were the last line of defense. How does it feel? Knowing you saved the entire eighth-grade class?"

Jeffrey spins me slowly around. It offers me glimpses of the rest of the room. Not visions of the future. No ill-fated omens. I'm just seeing the present moment, the here and now. DeSean and Sophie are taking a selfie nearby. My cousin Mary is laughing with Tatyana about something. Skyler and Avery are chatting comfortably with their respective Patricks. Other students twirl around the dance floor or hover by the snack table. It's one of those sprawling, perfect moments.

It reminds me of Grammy. Sometimes she'd walk over to the couch and snatch the remote. She'd aim it at Mom and me, jamming her finger down on the pause button. She would always tell us that she wished that was one of her powers. The ability to pause those perfect, shining moments in the present that feel like they *should* go on forever. I'm thinking about all of that when Jeffrey leans in and brushes my forehead with a kiss. I lean into him a little and whisper my answer.

"I guess you could say I feel like the *luckiest* girl in the world."

CHAPTER TWENTY-NINE

Loose Ends

The next few days at school are *normal.*

I never realized how much I liked that word. I guess I've spent so much of my life knowing that I would be anything but normal that I kind of overlooked the concept. It's super underrated, though. A few days pass without self-writing journals or luck-infused cookies, and I feel like I'm a regular student again. My most difficult task during that time? Algebra.

It is a little awkward being in a hallway with Patrick Bell. Most people still think he's cool, even if his excessive-sweating incident slowed the buzz. He still starts on the basketball team. His life *isn't* ruined. But that doesn't stop him from throwing dirty looks my way every time we pass each other in the hallway. After all, he's the only one besides my crew who knows what happened at the dance. He might not have any idea *how* it happened. And really, I know that he'd never tell a soul. It's tough to prove that someone used magic to break a lucky streak you were on because of special cookies. That sounds more like a fever dream than anything.

I know that I could ignore him, but the idea of having a rival doesn't sit right with me. I don't want there to be someone who walks around our school, talking bad about me to their friends. I wait a week before making the decision that I think Grammy would make. Sometimes you just have to talk things out, no matter how awkward it is.

Patrick Bell is sitting in the hallway after school, waiting for basketball practice to start. He's got headphones on, and his new shoes—which were so shiny the week before—look a little scuffed. That's unlucky. I walk straight up to him. He sees me and shoves up to his feet, like we're about to duel each other or something. I hold out one finger and reach into my book bag for a small plastic container. I asked Skyler to help me out the day before. I offer the container to Patrick.

There are three pristine cookies inside.

"Consider this a peace offering," I say. "There's no good luck or bad luck in them. Just chocolate chips, and I think a few M&M's. Skyler made them. We just wanted to say . . . sorry."

He looks both surprised and wary. Like this could be a trap.

"How do I know they're not poisoned or something?"

I roll my eyes. Opening the container, I perform a demonstration, taking a huge bite of one of the cookies. It tastes absolutely delicious. Skyler suggested cooling them overnight in the fridge. She said all the ingredients mix better that way, and she was right.

I offer him the container again. "See? No poison."

Patrick still looks suspicious. "Whatever. Why would I take anything from *you*?"

"Hey. I said I was sorry, but you know, the other night

didn't have to happen. I tried to fix things when it was just you and me sitting in that bakery. All you had to do was eat the cookie. I gave you a chance to save everyone. It's not like I *wanted* to embarrass you."

"So you admit it!" He starts looking around like he's hoping a teacher is close enough to hear the confession. "You . . . you did something to me!"

"Yes, I did. But here's the thing, Patrick. What I did the other night? It wasn't just to save the rest of the eighth grade. What I did the other night saved *you*, too."

"What are you talking about?" His tone is full of annoyance. "You said I was lucky. That I'd be really lucky for the rest of my life. What'd you save me from? Being the best?"

"No. I saved you from a life where nothing you did actually mattered."

Mary explained all of this to me the other day, when I started feeling bad about what we'd done to Patrick. She told me that I helped him a lot more than I hurt him. Patrick has the same semiconfused expression I probably had when I first talked through it.

"Think about it," I say. "All that extra luck? Sure. You would make every shot and maybe you'd get to play basketball in college and win all the random shoe giveaways. But you would have spent the rest of your life not knowing if you were actually good at anything. There's no way you could know if you did something with your own skill, or if it just worked out because the luck was helping you. Do you really think that you could live that way, Patrick? I know the good luck was fun for the last few months. I'm sure it was nice . . . being liked by everyone at school."

His face falls when he hears that. His eyes stay pinned to his shoes. It's like he's already accepted the idea that everyone is going to stop liking him now.

"But that's my point, Patrick! If you give them a chance, people will like the *real* you. Do you really want people to spend time with you just because . . . you're lucky? Or do you want them to spend time with you because . . . you're you? A part of why I don't feel bad about what I did is because I think the *real* you was worth saving. Even if you weren't particularly nice to me the other day . . ."

His eyes flick back up. I'm sure the last few days have been very different for him. Without every little detail falling neatly into place. Without everyone at school drooling over him. It's probably been hard. For a second, he doesn't say anything. And then he reaches out to take the cookies.

"Skyler made you those because we just wanted you to know that it's going to be okay. Really, it's going to be better than okay, because you'll know that everything happening in your life from here on out is *real*. You get to decide what happens next. It's up to you, Patrick."

When he doesn't meet my eye, I turn around and start walking away. I find myself hoping he'll shout for me to wait up. That he'll come running over and apologize. None of that happens. As much as I want the storybook ending where everyone becomes friends, Patrick's silence reminds me of something Grammy told me on the greenway last year.

We cannot control how the world sees us. All we can do is use our magic to the best of our ability. We must be wise and gracious and kind. It is the only way to make the future a better place.

Grammy's right. I can't control how Patrick Bell sees me. All I can do is wield my magic responsibly, and sprinkle in some kindness along the way. Not to mention the free cookies. Who doesn't like free cookies? I walk down the hallway and feel the guilt I've been carrying around start to slip off my shoulders.

I did my best, and that's more than enough.

After making my peace with Patrick Bell, there's just one more missing ingredient. Mary stuck around for most of her school break. She and Tatyana really hit it off. But when the two of them weren't hanging out, Mary was knee-deep in research. She went through every photo album and notebook that Grammy had made or kept over the years, up in our attic. Sometimes I'd hear her coming down the ladder late at night, coughing from all the dust swirling in the air up there. It took her almost a week to find what she was looking for.

Now we both exchange nervous glances as we wait for our guest to arrive.

The whole scene is set. I have cookies in the oven. An old recipe of Grammy's that I thought I'd try out. Mary has placed the Cleary Family Guide Book—along with her notes and research—on the table in the living room. We both hear a light *knock, knock*. I stand up, smooth my sweatshirt, and walk to the door.

Skyler Dawkins is waiting on the front porch. It's the first time I've seen her since visiting the Spellbound Bakery to pick up Patrick's cookies. I kind of expected her to fall in with our group, the way that Jeffrey did last year. But the opposite happened. Ever since the dance, I haven't seen her at school at all, even though I know we have a few points in our day where we *should* cross paths. It took talking to Mary to figure out she's been avoiding us—or specifically, avoiding me.

"Hey, Skyler. Come on in."

She offers a nervous smile. It fades quickly when she spies Mary on the couch. Her eyes dart between us. "Look. I know what you're gonna say—"

"But I've already decided," Mary cuts in. "Thanks, but no thanks. I'm *done* with magic."

Skyler's eyes narrow. I realize those must be the *exact* words that she was about to say. Mary smiles at the look on the girl's face. "There was a seventy-three percent chance you'd say that," she explains. "There's also a hundred percent chance you're going to sit down. And a forty-seven percent chance that you'll actually listen to us."

I can't help smiling as Skyler heaves a huge sigh. She can't resist, though. She crosses the room, intentionally sitting on the very far end of the couch, away from Mary. I take the comfortable armchair across from her. The Cleary Family Guide Book is sitting on the table between the three of us.

"Thanks for coming, Skyler," I say. "Are you doing all right?"

She half snorts. "Oh, I'm great. I almost ruined the lives of the *entire* eighth grade. Not to mention I'm so nervous that I might put magic into everything I'm baking that I've burned like six batches this week at work. So yeah. You could say I'm doing pretty great."

Mary nods knowingly. "Celia and I both get it, Skyler. She spent her entire seventh-grade year saving someone's life over and over. I have probabilities popping into my thoughts so often that, unless I'm out on the river rowing, I get a migraine at the end of every day. Trust me. If anyone understands what you're going through, it's the two of us."

Skyler chews on her lip but says nothing.

"The other day I told you that you're a Charmist," I say. "It's important to know what you are and what kind of magic you can do, but it's also important to know *who* you are. Mary's been doing some research this week. . . ."

My cousin reaches over. There's a small folder beside the family guide book. She opens it, turning so that Skyler can see the contents. I spot a flicker of confusion, followed by recognition. Mary showed me the same picture earlier. I had the same reaction. It features a group of siblings. They all look like they're in high school or college. I recognized Grammy instantly. She looks younger and a little cooler? It's hard to tell what qualifies as cool during this time period. The girl who's tucked under her arm, though, looks impossibly similar to Skyler.

"Who is that?"

"We're pretty sure that's your grandmother. Her name is Uva. At least . . . you look *exactly* like her. It's hard to imagine that the two of you aren't related. Same nose, same eyes, same chin. You said you've never met your grandmother?"

"Not on my dad's side, no. I don't know. I always asked about it when we were little, but my mom never told me anything." Skyler shrugs. "I kind of just . . . stopped asking."

Mary nods. "Well, I'm not sure what the nature of their relationship is, but Uva was *our* grandmother's sister. Which means . . ."

"You're our second cousin," I say with a smile. "You're a Cleary, Skyler."

She's shaking her head. I can't tell if it's in disbelief, or if she just doesn't like the idea of being one of us. Mary and I discussed this next part for a while. I've been kind of possessive of the Cleary Family Guide Book ever since I learned it existed. That feeling only grew when Grammy died. The book felt like the one place I could go to find her thoughts and words. The only way I could still spend time with my favorite person in the world. But the past month has taught me she's still very much with me—in head and heart. Besides, it's time to invite a new member into our family. Mary eventually convinced me. You can't invite someone without a proper housewarming gift. I heft the book up from the table and hold it out to her.

"We want you to have this, Skyler. Not forever, but for as long as you need. There's a lot in there. Our family—your family—has been creating that book for generations. We aren't going to force you to use magic. No one can do that. But the two of us were so lucky to grow up knowing our Grammy. She taught us everything she could. Told us stories. Every time one of us had our 4,444th day, it was this big celebration of a life that we'd already been taught how to live."

Skyler reaches out to take the book. It's hard to let it go, but when she tugs at the edges, I don't resist. Instead, I smile down at her the way Grammy would smile at me.

"Read through it. Look at all the notes our family has left over the years. If you decide that this life isn't for you?" I shrug, knowing she'll never be able to leave this world behind. "We won't stop you. But if you *do* want to know more about being a seer, Mary and I will be here to help."

Skyler no longer looks like someone who was tricked or trapped. She runs a gentle hand over the worn cover of the family guide book. I can tell that she's thinking about everything. It will take time for the joys of our magic to outweigh the fear of what happened this year. I'm pretty sure if anyone can win Skyler over, though, it'll be Grammy—and the rest of the eclectic Clearys who left their legacy in those pages. The three of us sit in respectful silence until Skyler's nose crinkles slightly. She leans down a little and sniffs the book.

"What's that smell?"

"Tradition," Mary and I both answer at the same time.

That has the two of us belly laughing as we realize that we both probably asked the same question of Grammy—and that she answered in the exact same way. Now we've taken her words and echoed them to a brand-new seer. Our laughter is contagious. Skyler breaks out into a huge grin and starts flipping through the pages. Even though we just told her to take all the time she needs, she can't resist firing off questions about different spells and the other types of seers.

I settle into my seat, listening as Mary retells a story about one time when she used her gift to cheat every game at the local arcade. She kept hitting jackpots and set the record for most tickets won in an hour, all so she could win a stuffed bear that wouldn't even fit through their front door.

As I listen to them talk, I see a flicker of movement. The door into Grammy's room is open. I can see her rocking chair. I know that it's empty. I know there's no magic that can bring back the dead—but for a brief whisper of a moment, the past drapes itself over the present. Grammy is sitting there, sporting her mysterious smile. She winks at me just as the light from the window flickers. And then there's just a rocking chair. Empty but never *really* empty. I know it still holds the shape of her memory. I can't help smiling. Grammy, wherever she is, must be delighted.

She once told me that it was an honor to watch more magic come into this world because the world has precious little of it left. Even though Skyler and Mary have drifted into a conversation about their favorite TV shows, I know *this* is what she meant. I kind of felt like the world had lost most of its magic last year when Grammy passed away. It was almost like a color had been completely erased from existence. Every tree stripped of its green, every leaf dulled to a lifeless gray.

I never thought the world would *feel* as magical as it once did with her in it.

I still miss her, and I'll probably miss her every day for the rest of my life, but adding a new member to the family has the world feeling bright with magic—full of possibility. I know that Grammy would celebrate this, which means I want to celebrate this. I reach for the remote.

"Those shows are good," I say. "But have either of you watched *Vampire High*?"

I cross over and plunk on the couch between the two of them. It doesn't take long to get the first episode cued up. "Should we eat a snack?" Mary asks. "Popcorn?"

"Oh! The cookies! Shoot, I forgot about the cookies!"

I scramble off the couch, sprinting across the room. I just know they're going to be burned to a crisp. But as I skid to a stop, I see the oven is already off. The cookies are cooling on the stovetop. Mom bustles in from the garage. "Hey, honey! Pulled those out for you earlier. I'm going to be collecting my fee now."

She steals one before heading up to her room. I return with a plate for the girls. For some reason, there's an echo of déjà vu to this moment. I can't put my finger on why until we're halfway through the first episode of *Vampire High*. There's a chase scene through a busy marketplace. It finally hits me. The story about the seer that Grammy used to tell me. The one who was so focused on predicting the futures of others that she accidentally let her own house catch on fire.

I realize that there are a lot of missing details to that story. There's no mention of whether or not she has a family. We don't find out where she lives or what kind of magic she uses. Maybe it's not really a lesson about balancing magic and life after all. If it was just up to me, I'd probably get distracted too and forget that I was baking cookies and burn our townhome to the ground.

But it's not *all* up to me.

I have Mom to keep me grounded. I have Jeffrey pointing me the right way, like a finely tuned moral compass. I have DeSean and Sophie and Avery and Tatyana, like stars in a night sky to guide me. I have my cousins, too, who each have their own powers and wisdom.

Maybe that story is all about surrounding yourself with people who are smart enough to turn the oven off when you forget to. Maybe it's a story about how a seer needs *people* if they want to avoid complete disaster. If that's the lesson—I think, snuggling in closer to Skyler and Mary—then I know that I'll be ready for just about anything.

Acknowledgments

I am grateful to the team at Aladdin for believing in me and this series. I am especially indebted to Anna Parsons for seeing these books as worthy of having a place on the shelf. People get to enjoy Celia Cleary's stories because of your vision. Thank you to everyone at the team who played a role in bringing this project to life. I'm always so humbled to collaborate with you all. Another huge shout out to my agent Kristin Nelson. You're always a phone call away. Always supportive. Always fighting for me. Thank you for everything.

This book is all about middle school. It's about the drama

that comes from a doomsday experience—but sometimes, middle school can really feel like a doomsday experience all on its own. I remember walking around the halls of Lufkin Road Middle School with nervousness radiating out from me with nuclear force. I was always worried about what people would think about me, worried about whether they really liked me or not. Middle school is a time where so many people are just trying to navigate life and figure out who they are. This final shout out is for all the middle schoolers out there who are trying to find their voice, trying to be brave—which often just means they're trying to be themselves in a world that would rather they be something else. This book is for you. No matter what kind of doomsday scenario you feel like you're facing, there's always a way through. All it usually takes is a little bit of luck and the right team to help you face it.

About the Author

SCOTT REINTGEN is a former public school teacher and still spends summers teaching middle schoolers dark fiction and fantasy at Duke Young Writers' Camp. The birth of his children has convinced him that magic is actually real. He lives in North Carolina, surviving mostly on cookie dough and the love of his wife, Katie. Scott is the author of the Nyxia Triad and Ashlords series and *A Door in the Dark* for young adults, as well as the Talespinners series and *The Problem with Prophecies* for middle graders. You can follow him on Facebook and Instagram, and find him on Twitter @Scott_Thought.